#IREMEMBER

BY: ASHLIE GIBBS

"AS LONG AS THERE IS A STORY TO TELL, THERE IS ALWAYS A BOOK TO WRITE"

Special thank you to everyone who helped make this book possible.

#THERAPY

Columbia, South America...

Valerie loaded her nine millimeter weapon and locked it into her waist holster. "Are you sure you want to enter the premises this way?" Ray asked. Originally, Ray trained Valerie when she was recruited to the agency, teaching her the deadliest skill sets to survive and kill. He did it not knowing she would surpass him in the field. Valerie laughed and shook her head at his doubt, "How many of these missions have we done together?"

Ray loaded his weapon, "More than I can count."

"How many times have I been wrong?" Valerie asked with an arrogant undertone.

"None." Ray smiled, "I trust you." The attraction and chemistry between the two was evident the second they met.

The truck stopped and the team jumped off. As they stepped into the forrest the rain came pouring down. "I am going after the target!" Val whispered to Ray.
Valerie parted from the group and maneuvered up the side wall of the mansion towards the balcony door. The rain drenched her hair and clothes as she moved towards the glass doors eyeing the target. Valerie raised her weapon with her finger on the trigger. But, before she could fire she paused. Her body tighten up with sharp pain. "Pop pop!" Two shots. Valerie fell to her knees in shock as droplets of blood mixed with puddles of rain water on the concrete balcony. She fell back and her head hit on a concrete pillar knocking her unconscious.

Present Day…

Valerie Cabria wasn't your average twenty something female. Not since her accident leaving her with memory loss…for the last several months she had been haunted by nightmares of what seemed to be another version of herself. Valerie stood in her master bathroom rinsing her face. "Honey are you okay?" Eric asked. She looked at herself in the mirror, and Eric awaited her answer as he stared at the two healed gun shot wounds on her back.

"Um, I'm fine," she lied.

"No, you're not, did you have another nightmare?" he asked. Some time between her accident and now she met and married Eric. Some would say it was rushed, others would say it was a mistake. But her family wanted her taken care of.

Val looked at him in the mirror, and nodded. "I don't understand the woman in my nightmares or even what is happening to her."

"I think you need to take your job's offer and talk to someone." Eric suggested while leaning against the wall. "This has been happening for a while now."

Val turned around and leaned against the sink. "Okay." She sighed but in her heart she was against therapy because it gave her the sense of being weak.

The following morning, Valerie took off from work and drove downtown to Los Angeles. As far as she knew, she worked as a city liaison. Ever since her accident the job has insisted she speak to a therapist. Funny, they had one already designated for her. Who knew the city has a therapist on stand by.

"Valerie why don't you tell me why you're here?" The therapist asked.

Val tapped her fingers against her leg as a coping mechanism. "I keep having these nightmares where I die." She started to explain her emotions, though she herself didn't understand them.

"Tell me about them."

"I am holding a weapon. A gun. It was like I was on a mission. I don't even know how to shoot a gun but it felt…" Valerie looked at her hands and created a fist, "so natural."

"Well, you did have an accident."

Val nodded, "I was on lunch walking down the sidewalk and tripped and hit my head. That's what they told me when I woke up."

"Yes, and your husband Eric?"

"What about him?" Valerie asked, confused as to why her husband was being brought into the session.

"How is he responding to this? I assume you have shared this with him."

Valerie took a deep breath, "He's worried about me."

"Tell me Valerie…" The therapist lowered her pen, "Is Eric the only family you have?"

"No. I have an older brother and a mother and father that live in the area."

"Do you spend time with them?"

"My mom and dad, yes. My brother and I are at odds right now." Valerie shifted her body uncomfortably on the couch.

"Why?"

"Why is this important? What does my brother have to do with me holding a gun?" Valerie hated talking about her brother and bringing up their relationship.

The therapist stopped her, "Because your relationships will help you move past your trauma."

Valerie placed her hands on the edge of the couch cushion and looked at the therapist, "My brother doesn't say much to me, and I don't to him…that is all you need know."

"So, you feel that your brother neglects his relationship with you, his only sister that nearly died."

"It makes me angry, but again that doesn't explain my nightmares."

"That is what we are going to figure out Valerie." The therapist tried to reassure her.

A few hours later Valerie went home. She and Eric lived in a gated suburban neighborhood outside the city. Eric found the newly built home, thinking it was a great way for her to heal from the trauma. She walked inside and smelled food as her husband was making her favorite seafood pasta. He always cooked for her as a way to show her comfort.

"How was your session?" Eric asked.

"It was a good start. She asked about my brother."

"Okay. Don't you think it's time you and him spend some one on one time together to mend your relationship."

"I love him but not visiting me once in the hospital is low. I told you how I feel about my brother will not impact your close friendship with him."

"I know." Eric said while kissing her cheek, "How about a glass of wine?" He went to the cabinet and pulled out two glasses, dropping one.

Valerie caught it between her fingers inches away from hitting the wooden floor. Eric froze and looked at her. "Now those are some serious reflexes babe!"

"Ugh...here." she said while handing him the glass. "I've been back in the gym since I was cleared." Valerie constantly had small flash backs of memories during the day that would deliver confusion. She always kept seeing one man…

Val and Ray were sitting on the floor in a small living room drinking wine and laughing. "We can't keep this hidden." Ray said sipping from his glass alluding to their secret relationship.

"You think they know me and you are at a vineyard right now?" Val asked with a smile.
"Nope. We disappeared."
Val leaned in and kissed him shifting the sheets to cover their bodies. "If I had to disappear with anyone. I am glad it's with you."
"Good." Ray smiled.

"Eric did we ever go to a vineyard years ago?" Valerie asked while sipping her wine.
Eric poured some pasta onto the plate, "No. We talked about it, right before the wedding last year but never did."

Valerie sat at the island kitchen counter as her eyes scrambled. She was pulling a memory from years ago. All she can recall since her accident is her few month long relationship with Eric before the two married. So, who is this other man?

Eric placed the plate in front of her breaking her thoughts, "You should eat something babe."

Valerie began to realized her dreams, nightmares, memories all have meaning. The question is what and who are the people in them? A few days later Eric got wind he would need to travel. "How long is your business trip?" Valerie asked as she watched Eric pack a suit case and rummage around the bedroom looking for small essentials. "Just a couple weeks. You know how running my family business still makes me travel." Eric answered while kissing her forehead. "So, call me every night. I want to make sure you're okay. I hate leaving you like this."

"I'll be fine, I have another therapist session soon. You worry too much…"

"…and dinner tonight?" He asked hinting at Val seeing her brother.

"I will be fine! You worry too much." Valerie repeated herself.

Eric zipped his suitcase and Valerie walked with him outside to his car. She glanced around and saw other housewives watching the two of them. They lived in a neighborhood full of nosey married women. "Kiss me..." he said while opening his arms.

Valerie walked over to him as he towered over her. She was 5'5 petite and her body was toned with light muscular definition. She leaned her head back allowing her shoulder length loose curly hair to fall back from her face just enough for him to softly kiss her lips. "I love you," he whispered.

"I love you too."

"I will call you when I land." Eric climbed into his car after placing the suitcase in the trunk.

He drove off and Val continued to look at the ladies as they stared at her. She didn't understand why the women paid so much attention to her and Eric.

"So glad to see you recovering Val after your little accident." Amy, Valerie's neighbor across the street commented. Amy's husband was an investment banker and constantly away. Good 'ol Amy always stopping to speak though her comments were insulting and stunk of jealousy.
"Thanks." Valerie responded showing no reaction to her words.
"Let me get out your way. You gotta stay in shape for Eric. 6'0 dark brown hair and green eyes successful man...you don't want another women swooping in there! He is a sexy guy!" She laughed.

Valerie waved at Amy and her friends before walking inside the house to change her clothes for dinner with her family. When she arrived at her parent's house she stayed inside the car for a few extra minutes anxious to see her brother.

Every call and text message ensued an all out word battle and calling of names. "Val! Honey you are looking better and better!" Grace yelled from the door as she saw her daughter walking up the sidewalk.

"Hey mom," she responded with tremble in her voice.

"Come inside sweetie we are waiting for you." Grace, her mother guided her inside the house.

Valerie saw her father and brother watching television. "Hey sweetie, you are getting better." Val's father Craig said while kissing her cheek. Valerie smiled at her father, but lost her smile while looking at her brother, Liam. "This is how it's going to be, just staring at each other?" He asked under his breath while standing up.

"Oh you see me now?" Val said while walking away towards the dinner table.

"Enough you two." Grace fussed. They all sat down at the dinner table and began passing around the food and filling their plates.

"How has work been Val?" Grace turned her attention back to her only daughter. Her parents knew little about her city liaison position. They knew even less when it came to Val's past life when she left home at 19 years old.

"Um, progressing and getting easier." Val said while pushing around her mashed potatoes.

"…and the nightmares?" Craig asked. Valerie lowered her fork and looked at her parents with a sigh; "Getting worse."

"Oh honey." Grace responded with remorse.

Liam sighed and shook his head. "You're recovering Val and that takes time."

"I didn't know you were a doctor Liam." Valerie responded snarky.

"Lets not do this you two!" Grace yelled, while looking at both of them.

She's the one with the huge problem" Liam shot back with a glare in Val's direction

"How is she doing?" Valerie asked hinting at how much of a womanizer her brother was. He always found a way to put his relationship before his family.

"Who?!" Liam raised an eyebrow.

"The woman you deserted me for while I was in the hospital!" Their voices grew louder and so the sibling rivalry escalated.

"You're not going to blame this on me." Liam picked up his dish and left the table.

Valerie jumped up and followed him into the kitchen, "You said you wanted to talk about it don't punk out and run away!"

"I said I would, but not if you're going to gang up on me!!"

"You did! You never came once!" Val yelled as tears fell from her eyes. She was angry with Liam but mostly hurt. Grace and Craig continued to sit at the dinner table as their children argued in the kitchen. "We should stop them." Grace whispered.
"No, they need to talk it out."

Liam sighed and calmly spoke, "And how would you know Val, you were in a coma; I did come see you. I sat there and watched while you were in a coma. Have you had to watch some one lay there in non-responsive position in another dimension? It's easier said then done."
Valerie pursed her lips fighting back tears. "No Liam."
"Well, I did!" He reached out to comfort her, but Val gripped his wrist. Twisted his hand and flipped him onto the floor. Liam coughed and grabbed his side as he slowly stood up, "What the hell!!!"

Valerie backed up and shook her head, "I'm so sorry!"
"When did you....how did you..." Liam was in shock while leaning against the counter for support.. and looking at his your sister in wonderment.

Valerie left her parent's house with little to no words. When she got home she stripped out of her dress and climbed into the bath tub full of hot water. "What did I do? Where did that come from?" She whispered to herself as her mind raced and she closed her eyes rested her head on the ledge of garden style tub…

"Come on take a swing!" Ray yelled. "I don't want to hurt you."
Ray lowered his gloves and stared at her. "Val, you have a good punch but I doubt you can hurt me."

Val swung at him and he caught her, "Nice try…" he whispered in her ear.

She turned around and faced him. "What happens now?" she asked.

"I take on this mission, and you continue focusing on growing and training." Ray answered.

Val shook her head, snatched off her gloves and sat down on the bench in the middle of the gym. Ray walked over sipping some water from a bottle and sat next to her, "Don't act like that! Don't you know I worked hard for this…"

"I hate it." Valerie responded fighting back all her feelings. There were so many situations that kept them both from having what they wanted.

"You have worked hard as well. You know the job would never keep us together." Ray added, hoping she take a

logical approach to controlling her emotions.

She touched his face, "Don't forget about me."

"How could I? Valerie, some of the best moments in my life were with you." Ray commented, "Here..." he took off his wrist band and signaled for her to take off her chain hanging around her neck. "Take my wrist band, I will take your chain...now we can never forget about each other."

"That's cute," Valerie laughed while putting on his wrist band.

"You're cute." he said while kissing her, "Don't ever doubt what you mean to me."

Valerie opened eyes and jumped out of the tub and ran to her jewelry box dripping water on the bedroom carpet. She started digging in some of the smaller compartments and there it was a black and dark brown beaded wrist band. The exact one Ray gave her in the memory. "Oh my gosh…" she said while holding it up placing it on her arm and then quickly removing it.

Valerie had a light routine with work. She did most of the work and phone calls from home, so it was very rare she was in the office. She had settled into a pattern; every morning she would make herself an iced coffee with a splash of cream; walk outside and look up and down the street, and then find a spot in the living room by the window to begin her work for the day.

Her phone rung and the screen illuminate with Eric's name. She forgot to call him after dinner. "So.. how was it? You didn't call me."

"I know babe, I am so sorry. It was eventful I accidentally attacked Liam."
"Accidentally attacked?"

"Yes, It was like a natural reaction, totally unexplainable, like when I caught that wine glass the other day." Val commented. As Eric started talking Valerie began to think about the bracelet and drown out his voice. She stared at her rose bushes in the back yard wondering why the color scheme was wrong, one set was blue and white tint.

"Where did you find this place?" Valerie asked while looking through the empty newly purchased home. Eric wrapped his arms around her waist and kissed her neck, "Newly developed gated community. Perfect environment to finish your rehab on your own accord."

Valerie turned around and kissed him,
"I love it…but I have to check out the
master bathroom!"

"You go ahead babe, I will get some of
these boxes!" Eric yelled. He walked
out to the trunk and looked around to
make sure he wasn't watched. He dug
into one of the boxes to grab a wooden
box. His phone buzzed with a message,
'bury it so she will never find it.'

Valerie was drowning out Eric's voice
while staring profusely into the
backyard, "...You and him have to work
it out honey. You can't keep battling like
this at family dinners." Eric added while
noticing silence on the other end,
"Honey…are you listening?"
"You are right. Honey I will call you
back." Valerie hung up the phone and
walked out of the kitchen into the
backyard.

A group of agents like herself stood in the briefing room listening to their lead. "This is one of the most dangerous missions you will be on." Val looked at Ray, "We are in this together." "You got my back and I have yours." Valerie nodded, "Okay, I'm down." She went home that night and sat on the couch staring at a dark brown wooden box. "Always have insurance Valerie." she said to herself while placing it amongst her things in her apartment.

Val gripped the shovel and started digging up the blue white tint rose bush that was in the center of the red ones. "Something isn't right!" She said to herself.

After 10 minutes of digging she hit something hard. She got on her knees and dug in the dirt and pulled out a medium size dark brown wooden box.

Valerie regained her strength while looking around making sure no one saw her. She picked up the box and took it inside the house.

She placed the box in the center of the kitchen floor and opened it to see passports, money, two guns, and papers. Valerie brushed her hair away from her face in shock. "Now how did you get out there?"

"Practicing for this last mission?" Ray asked while loading up his weapon at the gun range.

Valerie lowered her pistol and looked at him, "Yea. Something about this isn't right."

"Like what?"

"I don't trust something about this mission."

"But you trust me right?"

"This is more than just trusting you Ray, it is about the safety of this mission." Valerie added.

"When has a mission not been safe Val? When have I ever not had your back?" Ray said after taking two shots at the target.
"That is not what I meant...It's not you, it's this overall mission." Valerie added while looking into his eyes.
Valerie lifted the gun and Ray slid behind her gripping her waist.
"Breathe, that's how you hit your target," Ray whispered in her ear.

Valerie loaded the pistol that was lying in the box. Her mannerism with handling a weapon was natural for her. The feel and touch of a weapon triggered something…she knew how to use it. Then she saw a letter written and signed by her. The main words that caught her eyes...**Don't trust anyone.**

Valerie found herself asking triple the questions she did before. In order to get answers she needed the therapist.

The following day Valerie was back on the couch. Val so glad you returned for another session," the therapist commented.

Valerie nodded, "My husband seems to think I can get something out of this."

"Have you had anymore nightmares since our last visit?" The therapist asked with her pen and paper ready.

Valerie paused, she was hesitant to speak her mind. Could she actually trust this woman? "Not really." she answered choosing not to.

"Really?" the therapist was shocked, "None?"

"I think things are calming down. I just wish I knew more about my accident." Valerie began to play stupid, "Is it possible that this is all I will remember?"

"Well Valerie, you hit your head and they believed it caused acute amnesia."

"Who is they?" Valerie wanted to be the one asking questions.

"The doctors at Cal Hospital."

"Valerie! Valerie hang in there!" Ray shouted while applying pressure to her gun wounds.

Valerie was in and out of consciousness asking, "Where am I...what...." Her voice faded in and out.

"Shh, save your strength." Ray turned to the driver, "We need to go faster she is losing too much blood!!!"

Valerie's breathing grew thin as she felt her strength leave her body, "Wha..." she whispered.

"We are minutes away from the hospital Val...please hang in there. I can't lose you." Ray said while holding her in his arms. His clothes covered in blood.

"Val!" The therapist fought to regain her attention, "Are you still with me?"

"Yea," Valerie said while coming back to reality.

"Are you sure you don't remember anything?"

"No. I should go." Valerie got up and left the room. The therapist watched her leave and immediately shut her office door. She picked up the phone and dialed a number. "Hello. Yes, I think we have a problem," she whispered.

As Valerie was driving she kept shaking her head trying to piece together moments of her life that included secret missions, a man named Ray, and a life she couldn't remember.

Desperate for answers she made a u-turn at the light and drove twenty miles out to Cal Hospital.

After parking she walked inside and went to the front desk. "Hello, I am looking to speak to a doctor, um my doctor." Val said to the receptionist.

"What is your name?"

"Valerie Cabria."

"You are looking for neurology. The Chief of surgery is Dr. Otter."

"Thank you." Valerie made her way through the hospital and slipped into hospital scrubs to blend in. She heard Doctor Otter's name and froze as she watched him go into his office. "Tracey hold my calls." He commented as he sat down in his chair. He looked up to see Val standing in front of him. "Valerie," he whispered remembering the day she arrived in the emergency room, and he was snatched for her surgery.

"I need a surgeon now!!" Ray yelled in the middle of the emergency room.
"I am the Chief of surgery, Dr. Otter..." He started, but was cut off by Ray's instructions, "Listen to me, she was shot and you will perform surgery on her now."
"We have to report all gun related..." Ray shook his head, "I don't think you understand, we are part of an agency working on a government mission. You

will perform surgery or I will
personally pay a visit to see your
family."
Dr. Otter looked at Ray in fear, and
then at his residents. "Sir, she is
crashing, we need to move now."
Dr. Otter put on some gloves and
nodded, "Prep OR 2 now!"

"You remember me," Valerie said while
looking at him.
"Yes I do."
"I need to know what happened to me."
Valerie demanded while stepping closer
to his desk.
"Val this isn't the place or time, you
could put both of us in danger." Dr.
Otter responded with the same fear from
that night.
"You are already in danger if I am
standing here! Tell me what happened to
me!"
"You really don't remember." Dr. Otter
froze, "You were brought into the

emergency room. Blood was every where. I um performed emergency surgery on your back for gun shot wounds, and treated your head injury."

"Gun shot wounds? They said I hit my head during a lunch break and I suffer from acute amnesia."

Dr. Otter shook his head, "That is only half true. They told me to leave the gun shot wounds out, and report only the part that you hit your head! They threaten my family!"

"Who is they!?"

"This government agency! I don't know, but you need to go now! I don't want them thinking I spoke to anyone about this."

Valerie sighed, "Give me a name."

"Val..."

"A name!" Valerie demanded.

"Ray...yea...Ray and a guy named Lucas." Dr. Otter added. "Now please leave!"

After getting what little information she could she left and drove home. She was hoping the information would ease her mind. It only frightened her to know that the man she was dreaming about was real. Later that night she stood in her shower as hot water hit her bruised body. She took her fingers to feel towards the middle of her back. She cringed while touching her scars from the gun wounds. It was clear that city liaison was a cover job for a much deadlier occupation.

"Honey how did I get these healed wounds?" Val asked Eric while looking in the mirror.
Eric walked up behind her, "You had an accident with a screw driver. You lost a lot of blood." Eric tried to provide an explanation without giving too much information.

She grabbed the towel and wrapped it around her body as she walked out of her bathroom to a man standing in the middle of her bedroom. She froze in place.

"Valerie..." he said in a deep calm voice. Valerie stared at him recognizing his face. The man from her memories, "Ray..."

They stood in front of each other in the middle of her bedroom. Her naked under a towel and him the man she has feelings for in her memories. He moved towards her but she took a few steps back tightening her towel. "I need to change…" Valerie said softly. Ray nodded and left the bedroom to go downstairs.

After changing into presentable clothes, Val poured hot water into a large mug and dipped in a tea bag. She took deep breaths as the water instantly turned brown.

"Um, here..." she said in a shaky voice while handing the mug to Ray.

"Thank you," Ray said while trying to appear harmless. He didn't mean to frighten her.

"Ray...?"

"Valerie..." Ray responded while intensifying his stare into her eyes. His gaze made her feel naked though this time she was wearing clothes.

The two always had an intense connection. They were once in love with each other. "Never let down your guard!" Ray shouted as the two sparred on the blue mat.

Valerie swung hitting him across the face and flipping him over. "Good," he responded.

Valerie turned her back and his arm gripped her neck picking her up, "Never take your eyes off your enemy." He responded while leaning backwards and flipping her onto the mat landing on top of her.

The two laid on the mat trying to catch their breath and staring into each other's eyes. Ray leaned in and kissed her, "God you're beautiful."

Valerie wrapped her arms around his neck caressing his back and passionately kissing him, "And you're sexy..." she laughed. It was her smile. He fell in love with her smile.

"Why are you here?" Val asked while standing up. Her heart yearned for him but her mind struggled to trust him.

"Your memories." Ray started, "I've been watching you from a far since your accident."

"You mean the one where I got shot?" Valerie asked.

"So you remember?"

Valerie shook her head, turned around and lifted up her shirt showing the gun shot wounds. Ray sighed, "I had to keep tabs on you to make sure you were okay."

"Stalking is illegal," Val made jokes in uncomfortable situations and this was one of them.

"You are my responsibility Valerie! What happened to you..."

"I don't know what happened to me!?" Val yelled, "My mind only replays bits and pieces!"

Ray laughed as he stood up, "You expect me to believe that you don't remember our moments together?"

Val backed up and shook her head, "Stop it."

"Every kiss, every touch, and every intimate..."

"Shut up!!!" Val yelled while moving further away.

Ray went to grip her neck and immediately, Val responded by slamming him against the counter with a small kitchen knife against his cheek.

"Never take your eyes off your enemy..." Val whispered while looking into his eyes. She remembered what he taught her.

Ray smirked, "The agency wants you to come in."

"No," Valerie answered while letting him go and putting the knife into the utensil drawer.

"Val, this isn't up for discussion. You have to come back in."

"Or what?"

"You will have to deal with me. You don't do so well with that so get it together," Ray commented. "Thanks for the tea. You should get the door, your brother is here." Ray finished.

The doorbell went off and Val heard her brother's voice. "Val! Open up I came by with take out. We should talk."

Valerie turned around and Ray was gone. She sighed because Ray was good at coming and going or was it all a figment of her imagination.

Valerie wanted to gather her thoughts before seeing her brother. Ray triggered an emotion, a lost love she hadn't felt since her accident. Val opened the front door for her brother who was holding two large brown bags. "I brought take out." He said lifting them up.

"I know, I heard you yelling on the porch." Val said while walking away leaving the door open for him.

"Look Val, I am here to make up for whatever it is I did to you." Liam said while following her into the kitchen.

"You don't even know what you did?!" Liam sighed and rolled his eyes, "I did visit you in the hospital!"

"No you didn't!"

"How would you know! You have amnesia remember!" Liam hit her with a low blow with his comment.

Valerie paused as she stared at her brother, "Be careful what you say to me big brother."

Liam laughed, "Are you going to flip me again?"

"No." She said while taking the food out of the bag, "I'll put you in the hospital." She said while staring deep into his eyes.

Liam stepped back a little sensing her seriousness in her words. "Val, I know I wasn't good when you were recovering from your accident..."

Valerie immediately saw an opportunity to learn as much as she could from her brother about what happened to her. Things were still hazy and with Ray out there watching her she still couldn't trust anyone.

"What did they say happened to me?" She asked.

Liam sat down at the island counter top, "That you had a head injury. That um you fell while on a lunch break."

"I fell… that's it and you believed that ?
Liam nodded, "Yeah, sort of but didn't
make sense, because you were bleeding
from your back."
"Who told you this?"
"Two of your coworkers who were there
that evening." Liam said recalling the
memory while eating.

*"Mom! I just got your call! What
happened to Valerie?" Liam asked
while rushing into the emergency room.
"She is bleeding really bad she is
unconscious. They won't let me see
her!"
Liam walked over to the room and a
man wearing all black who stopped
him. "Let me through that's my
sister!!" Liam yelled while pushing him
out of the way. He froze when he saw
Val with breathing tubes coming from
all over; preparing her for surgery.
"Liam?" A man asked.
"Yeah, who are you?"*

"I'm Ray, I work with Valerie."

"Seeing you like that, not knowing if you would live or die. It was a lot to handle Val." Liam said in a soft voice. Valerie reached over and touched her brother, "I didn't realize. I'm sorry."
"Yeah. But, some guy named Ray was there." Liam said picking up his initial thought.
"Ray?"
"Yeah, said he worked with you."
Valerie smiled, "This lo mein is good."
"Yeah we use to get lunch at this place all the time." Liam cracked a small smile on his face. Part of him was shocked that him and his little sister could share a moment.
"This place?" Val asked while holding up a menu.
"Yeah." Liam laughed, "The lo men is your favorite."

After having a surprisingly calm dinner with her brother Valerie took another hot bath. It was the only place she could think. She was at peace until she heard noises coming from down stairs. She slipped on some clothes loaded her gun and quietly walked down the stairs. She place the end of the gun against the back of a female's head, "You have two seconds to tell me who the hell you are." she whispered.

"I'm Casper! Please put the gun down!" She pleaded with her hand's up. Valerie lowered the gun and slammed Casper against the wall, "What are you doing in my house!?"

"Leaving you this..." she tried to speak and hold up a flash drive. "If you let me go I can explain."

Valerie released her. "I don't remember you Casper."

"Okay, that's fair. I am your technical analyst or was for all of your missions Valerie. We became friends."

"My analyst…my friend?"
"The agency uses analyst for team missions and um, yea we became friends." Casper explained.

Casper and Valerie sat at a table inside a local burger restaurant. "I created this for you. It is a fail safe." Casper said while sliding Val a black flash drive.
Valerie took it into her hand and stuck it away, "Good." Valerie said while looking at it, "There is something about this mission I don't trust Casper."
"It is strange Val. I will continue to do some digging."
"Be careful. I couldn't risk anything happening to my only friend." Valerie smiled.

"Casper!" Valerie said remembering who she was. "My only friend."
"Thank God, you scared me for a minute there." Casper gasped and patted Valerie

on the back. "When you got shot I went to the location and grabbed the flash drive to keep until you got better."

"Okay, so you are back?" Valerie asked.

"I am back to give this to you and hope it will help you. The agency is awaiting your arrival."

Valerie slowly walked away with thoughts on her mind.

Casper followed her, "You don't remember our missions together?" She asked as she started up her laptop to insert the flash drive.

"No. Not completely. It comes back in flashbacks; bits and pieces."

"Valerie, the mission in Columbia..." Casper began to recall.

Val cut her off, "Something went wrong."

"You were shot in the back twice.. I was tracing everything and hacked your original medical files before they were altered." Casper said while typing fast on the keyboard.

Valerie stopped stunned, "The only other person on the mission with me was Ray along with a few others from the team. But Ray was the only one who took me to the hospital."

"After that mission Lucas was made Director and Ray was promoted to Lead of the team." Casper explained the change in hierarchy at the agency.

"Casper I need to fully remember that mission or me getting to the bottom of things won't work."

"I agree, take a look at this. It was Lucas's idea to go on the mission. He set up the entire thing." Casper pointed at Lucas's signature on the flight documentation.

Valerie looked at Casper, "How did you get all of this?"

Casper laughed and fixed her glasses, "I was a hacker before they recruited me for an analyst position." She stopped typing, "I don't think they know that though…once a hacker always a hacker" she smiled slightly.

"Babe! I came home early! Where are you?" Eric yelled from the front door placing his suitcase down on the floor.

"Is that your husband?" Casper asked while shutting her lap top and sliding Valerie the flash drive.

Eric walked into the kitchen and stopped when he saw Casper and Val sitting at the table. Valerie stood up, "Betty, thank you so much for coming by and notifying me about those electrical changes." Valerie changed character to accommodate Eric's presence. Casper caught wind of the change and lipped, "Betty??"

Valerie's eyes widen and Casper answered, "No problem ma'am."

"Electrical changes?" Eric asked in a suspicious tone while looking at the two of them.

"The power went out babe and I was concerned." Val said with a smile. "So they sent out an electrician."

Casper cleared her throat, "Like I said ma'am, everything looks good here," Casper said while grabbing her things and leaving.

"You came home early."

Eric looked at the front door and back at Val, "Yea, I finished things at my parent's business."

"I missed you." she said while kissing him.

"Are you feeling okay?" Eric asked, feeling her immediate response was out of character.

"Yes," Come upstairs tell me about your trip.

The next morning Valerie snuck out the house in her running clothes. She sent one text message to Casper for them to meet at the local coffee shop. Valerie approached the end of the driveway and looked up to see Eric looking at her through the window. She smiled and waved to throw him off and he waved back. She started jogging down the street. Once she made it to the entrance she saw Casper inside sitting at a table typing on a black tablet. "Hey," Valerie said while sitting down in front of Casper.

"Well hello, I got your message friend! What's up?"

"I need you to tap someone's phone," Valerie responded.

"Oh wow…now thats a request. An easy one, but still an interesting request." Valerie sipped from the bottle of water sitting on the table, "It is but none the less important."

"Who am I spying on? Your therapist?" Casper asked.

"Yes, how did you know?"

"The agency assigned her. She isn't someone random. They picked her to monitor your memories during your sessions." Casper explained.

Valerie sipped some more water while thinking about her next move, "They want me back."

"Yea, you were the best agent they had. One of the most lethal."

"Then I will go back." Val agreed.

"You need to remember first! Clearly someone set you up and I am guessing they aren't happy you're alive." Casper exclaimed as the two left the table to walk outside the coffee shop.

Valerie stopped and looked at her friend, "I need to find the truth and it's back at the agency."

Casper nodded, "I will give you anything I can find."

"Thanks," Valerie said while jogging off.

Valerie made it back home sweaty enough to convince Eric she went on a full running trail around the neighborhood. Immediately she stripped down and took a shower to clean up. Her goal was to pay a visit to her therapist. After getting out of the shower she got a text message from Casper:

-Got something...

Valerie read the rest of the message on the phone and typed a response and deleted the text thread. She slipped on a white top and blue jeans to keep a more casual look.

"Headed out honey?" Eric asked while walking up behind her and kissing her cheek.

"Yes, I am going to see the therapist." she said while finish styling a bun in her hair. Eric walked out of the bathroom and Val loaded her gun placing it between her back and her jeans.

She drove downtown and parked a few blocks away ready to walk into the therapist office with a different agenda. She was vulnerable weeks ago, but now she is picking back up her skills and techniques. She just needed some final details before returning back to the beginning.

"Valerie, please have a seat! So glad you came back. You stormed out last time." The therapist said while shutting the door. Once she turned around Valerie was smiling at her.

"I am glad to be back." Valerie responded.

"Yes, so what do you want to discuss this time."

"I know you specialize in therapeutic memory loss using hypnotism."

"Valerie..."

"Don't lie to me. It's insulting."

"I do, but your memories..."

Valerie cut her off mid sentence, "You will help me remember them, or it is simple...you don't go home." Valerie threatened.

The therapist sat up in the chair and stared back at Valerie. She was nervous realizing who she was dealing with. Valerie moved to the edge of the seat and intensified her stare, "I know you know I am dangerous..."

The therapist nodded, "I do know…" she whispered with fear in her voice.

Valerie sent fear through the therapist body as she regained pieces of herself. Her determination to remember what happened and who she is was growing stronger. She was tired of lies and not having the truth. There was never a lunch accident, Valerie was shot, and now she intended to find out who set her up to die. It started there, with the therapist. Valerie laid back in the chair prepared to go back and fill in the blanks. She was ready to remember as much as she could. She took a deep breath and was ready to dive in.

"They say remembering is the easy part. It is living with the truth that haunts us," The therapist whispered. "Are you willing to live with the truth?"
Valerie was limp in the chair with her eyes shut. Her breathing was slow. "Yes..."
"Who is Ray?" The therapist asked while taking notes.
"Ray..." Val whispered as her eyes fluttered underneath her eye lids. Her mind raced back in time.

"I think you like working with me." *Ray said while smiling at her.*
"You're okay" Val joked while shrugging her shoulders.
Ray kissed Val's forehead and held her in his arms as the two laid in bed together. It was a love affair, a dangerous one. Both slept with guns underneath their pillows, but they never knew if it was because of the job or because they didn't consistently trust

one another. All they knew was they loved each other and would have the other's back.

"You and Ray are lovers…" The Therapist chimed in.
"No we were." Val corrected.
"No, you are. You speak of him in present tense meaning you still love him." There was a denial hidden in her words.
Val clinched the arm of the chair. "Val what happened on your last mission?" She asked.

Val and Ray were arguing as they constantly did. In his eyes everything was always her fault, and in her eyes he didn't understand her because he didn't want to.
"This…this is emotionally draining!" Ray yelled.

"It's emotionally draining because you can't be with me the way you want to!" Val yelled back with tears in her eyes. "It's a lot for me and then sometimes how you act..." He started.

"Do not! Do not try and make it seem like I am the only one with issues here." Valerie fussed.

"The mission Val..."

"I will always handle the mission." Val said with anger. She looked down at her phone to see a message from Casper - 'Trust no one...I think this mission is a set up.' Valerie looked up as she saw Ray walking away and pursed her lips with concern.

"Come on Val! The plane is ready to head to Columbia!" A teammate shouted.

"Val we have been over this. You are trained to know details, to analyze everything every second." The therapist fought to dig deeper. "What happened?!"

Before heading through the terrain, Ray sent a text message and stomped on his phone kicking it to the side. Val kept quiet, "I will take the side of the house."
"Barry will go with you." Ray noted.
"No, I will go alone." Val said while running away.

"They knew I would separate myself." Val whispered while recalling the memory.
Two pop noises, "Pop! Pop!" Val stood still, as the shots stung her body. She stared into the targets eyes and he wasn't surprised to see her at all.

"Open your eyes." The therapist noted. Valerie sat up and looked at her, "What if..."

"The man you fell in love with, betrayed you." The therapist finished. "Now it's time you talk to Ray." Valerie was struggling to swallow the truth that the man she loved, her first love, set her up to die.

Could it be true that Ray betrayed her? Why did he smash his phone during the mission? Valerie had so many questions. She sat at the table drinking some hot tea racking her brain around everything she gained from her session with the therapist. "Honey you alright?" Eric asked while grabbing a mug from the cabinet to join her.

#SECRETS

"Yea," Valerie's tone was low.
"How is therapy working out? Are you still having those nightmares about being shot?" Eric asked.
Val moved her attention to her husband realizing she never told him what her nightmares were about. She never mentioned being shot. "Therapy is coming along slowly. No nightmares." She lied. It was getting harder to trust the people around her.
Eric walked over and kissed her forehead, "I am glad you're getting better. I hate seeing you like this."
"I know," she responded as she got up and walked out of the kitchen pretending to go up the stairs.
Eric glimpsed around the corner and picked up his phone. "Lucas," he answered.

"How is she?" Lucas asked on the other end.

"Not suspicious that I can tell."

Lucas who was the newly appointed director of the agency shook his head, "Keep your eyes on her. She is good at manipulating. That is why she is one of the best."

"As long as she never finds out that I was part of her set up." Eric stammered. "That was the deal."

Lucas laughed, "Eric you got what you always wanted. The woman of your dreams. Now you have her. Just do your part and she won't find out. I'd hate for you to be her next target."

Eric sighed, "Yea." He laid his phone back down on the counter. He dropped his head thinking about how difficult things just became for him.

"What do you need me to do?" Eric asked as he stood in front of Lucas who was presenting a proposition.

"Get her to fall in love with you and marry her. I wanted her to die but obviously that didn't happen." Lucas explained while shaking his head, "So this is plan B."

"Why her?" Eric asked, "I don't get it..."

"You don't need to brother," Lucas said while looking at Eric, "You just need to know what move to make next. Do this, and you will get the $8 million to get out of debt."

Eric nodded as Lucas handed him an envelope of Valerie's information. He pulled out a picture of her. Lucas paused before walking away, "Brother, be careful. This isn't your average woman."

Eric laughed, "It's not like she is going to kill me."

"If she finds out, she will."

Eric sighed, "What did I get myself into..." he whispered to himself.

Meanwhile, Valerie leaned against the wall as tears ran down her cheeks. The man she woke up to and went to sleep with every night; the man who was there since her accident was involved in all of this. He was a link in whomever set her up.

The information was disheartening to learn. Valerie never thought that Eric would have played a role in her set up. But what part does he play? He isn't a trained operative otherwise he would have reacted differently to her behaviors. No, Eric plays a different part, and Lucas seems to be his handler. Eric was just a man. a regular everyday John, But how did he know Lucas, and what did he have on him?

"Val you're very quiet today. How are you responding to our last session?" The therapist asked while interrupting Val's thoughts.

Valerie was trained to be whomever the moment demanded she become. For years she has been working for a secret government agency, drafted straight out of high school and made her first kill before the age of 21. The agency made her a trained killer, and someone out there wanted her dead. In all of this, she found Ray, her trainer and the first man she ever loved. With him she let down her guard, with him she could be herself. Val smiled, "I am just thinking a little bit."

"About the memories you lost?"

"Yes, I have some of them back. I feel I am able to return to my profession." Valerie confessed.

The therapist lowered her pen, "…as the city liaison?"

"No…" Valerie laughed, "as a trained killer, but you knew that already." Valerie added as the therapist sat back in the chair with fear in her eyes. "That's why they hired you."

"I was hired by your employer." The therapist responded.

Valerie nodded and smiled, "Now we are getting somewhere."

"So what would you have me do Valerie? It is obvious that our intense memory session helped."

Valerie tossed her the flip phone she took from the therapist desk, "Call them and tell them I am choosing to come back."

"Okay," the therapist said while opening the phone.

Though she chose to return to the agency, she was still confused as to how to handle Eric. She wasn't in the mood to be fake and pretend that everything is perfect when she really wanted to tie him up and torture him for information. Valerie pulled up into the driveway at her home placing the car in park. She sat in there for an extra 10 minutes contemplating how to handle the information that fell into her lap.

She was torn because she didn't know who to trust. The more she regained her memory the more she was afraid to make her next move. Second-guessing herself was out of character for her. However, she was certain about one thing, she had to return back to the place where she was set up to be killed.

Ray carried Valerie into a safe house and sat her in the chair. He began searching for materials to help with her wound. "I am fine Ray we need to get out of here. I don't know how much longer we can last here in Spain."

"Shut up and let me think of what I need." Ray said while looking around, "because if I don't stitch you up, you won't make it back to the US." He

grabbed a safety pin and pulled thread from his shirt. Then he grabbed a bottle of alcohol and pulled out a match.
"Ray…"
He stopped and looked at her, "Why won't you let me in?" Ray asked as he helped stitch up her side that was bleeding.
Val looked into his eyes, he was the first man that wanted to be close to her, "because letting you in means you have the power to hurt me."
Ray pursed his lips as he closed up the wound, "Valerie…"
"I am always here for you. That makes me vulnerable…" Valerie confessed trying to mask her reactions to the pain of the wound.
"I am here for you too, maybe not right away, but I will be. You have to remember that." Ray added.
"Noted."

Val took a deep breath and put the car in reverse, backed out of the drive way. After driving a distance away she ended at the gun range outside the city. It was a very low key spot, and she needed to not be seen nor remembered. Hard because she was a woman, who was great at hitting her target. This gun range was one that many of the local military enlisted attended when they wanted to get away from base.

After paying for a weapon and bullets Casper showed up, "Hey! So, I got your message and can I say finding this place was not easy! What's up?"

"I need your help." Val said while loading her choice weapon. One of the more difficult guns to handle, an M4 MRK18.

Casper looked down at the gun and then at her, "You aren't going to shoot me are you? Because I swear I can be useful!"

Val raised her weapon and fired two shots at the target, "No."

"Okay..." Casper said awaiting for the reason why Valerie called her out to the gun range knowing she couldn't shoot with her.

"I need your help once I return to the agency. That is my next destination when I leave here." Valerie said while raising the gun and firing two more shots to hit her target in the center of the chest.

"Val, are you sure you're ready to come back. Things have changed since your injury."

"Someone alongside my husband Eric wants me dead. I survived this time, but I am guessing they won't stop until I am 6 feet under." Valerie responded with sternest in her voice. "My guess, they set up the job as city Liaison, made me think that I've been doing this for years. Hired a therapist to keep tabs on my memory."

Casper nodded in agreement, "I will help any way I can. Maybe you should get Ray in on this too."

Valerie lowered the weapon and took a deep breath, "The man I love pulled away from me and left. The man I married set me up and lied to me. I am in a dangerous amount of pain, and I have no intentions of staying this way." She fired off four shots to her target hitting it between the eyes each time.

Casper gulped, "What if hurting you was never their intention?"

"Just because hurting someone isn't intentional doesn't mean they won't feel pain. Are you in or not?"

"In." Casper answered. "I am your best friend, and if I can help catch the bastards who did this to you then I will."

"Good."

Parting ways Val went back home to change clothes before heading over to G36, the agency. The place where it all began for her. "Hey babe, I was just starting dinner." Eric shouted from the kitchen before Valerie could go upstairs.

She stopped halfway up the stairs mid-step, fighting the urge to retaliate or hold her peace after learning he might be involved in her assassination attempt. She took a few seconds to recall when they first met. She was just going through rehab therapy for her surgery.

*"How long have you been stuck here?"
Eric asked as he saw her sitting in the
chair waiting on her rehab instructor.
Bandages around her head, Valerie
turned her head to see a 6 foot tall dark
brown hair and green eyes guy smiling
at her. "Um…too long."
Eric sat down, "I feel you. I have a
cousin who comes here. You know what
you need?"
"What's that?"
"To get away" Eric suggested. "How
about coffee, we can start small."
Valerie looked into his eyes and smiled
back, "Coffee huh?"
"Only starting small." Eric flashed his
pearly white teeth and smiled back at
her.
"Sounds good." Valerie agreed.*

"Hey baby!" She said while kissing him
behind his neck and caressing his arms.

"Mmm someone is in a mood. I've missed you." Eric turned around and kissed her back.

"Are you cooking my favorite pasta again?"

"Yes, but I am also making BBQ chicken," Eric stated.

"I have to go into the office tonight and finish a project." Valerie noted while eating some of the chopped vegetables. Eric nodded while glancing at his phone that lit up showing Lucas' name. "That's fine. I will fix a plate and leave it for you."

"Thank you babe." Valerie said while walking away.

As soon as she left the kitchen Eric paused and then answered. "Hello?"

"Oh good, you're still alive." Lucas joked.

"Not funny, just finish your part of the plan and we can meet this week." Eric fussed before hanging up.

"Honey." Val interrupted.

Eric jumped, "Oh shit! You um, you scared me babe I thought you went upstairs."

"Bathroom…" Valerie answered, "Ugh maybe this weekend my brother can join us for dinner." Val suggested.

"Sounds like a plan."

Val went upstairs, changed clothes, loaded her weapon, and hid it underneath her clothes. She drove over an hour to the city border. After passing through countless security, she felt her heart rate rise. Flashbacks of coming to G36 ran through her mind.

She walked inside with security escorts before being greeted by Lucas, the newly promoted director of the agency. "Valerie, still as beautiful as ever."

"Always a pleasure Lucas." Val smirked. She lifted her arms as the guards searched her and removed her weapon.

"Precautions, I know you understand."
Lucas said while moving closer.

"I see you still don't trust me." Val said
with a smirk.

Ray stopped in the hallway when he saw
Val. "You came back," he said.

Valerie looked at the two of them, "Yes,
I am home, and I know there is a lot
waiting to be done."

Valerie walked through the halls
with Ray and Lucas remembering when
she was first drafted to the agency. She
lied and told her parents she was going
into the military, but was met by
someone to do something different. It
was hard for her to recall why she
decided to do it, maybe because college
wasn't going to be enough for her. She
needed something more.

In the Beginning...

"What's her story?" Lucas asked while staring at Valerie practicing combat amongst the other recruits.

Ray looked at her and then at him, "She is new."

"She has a fire inside of her, you have to watch out for those kinds. They never give up."

Ray nodded, "I agree, she doesn't give up easily."

Valerie rolled on the ground and flipped her opponent over her shoulder twisting his arm nearly breaking the bone. Immediately, he tapped out begging for her to release him. She stood up and dusted herself off. Ray walked up to her smiling, "You must be Val..."

"Yea, who are you?" Valerie asked.

"Ray, are you ready for a real practice run?" he asked while handing an assistant his keys and weapon.

"Let's do it." Valerie said while smiling at him.

They walked into the locker room and strapped up with vest and weapons.

"Okay our target is the mercenary with the green mask. There are several hostages. We want to take him alive alongside the hostages. Understand?" Ray asked while loading his weapon.

"Understood." She said while holstering her gun and knives. "Let's see who gets there first."

They went into the field house that was design by G36 for practice set up. They moved through the trees approaching a shack. The two separated and Ray's voice came over the radio, "Alpha I am going through the front, take the back."

Valerie dropped her head and laughed, "You have a sexy voice on the radio."

Ray laughed back, "Focus...Val."

"Of course, the back, copy."

She moved through the back and came upon heavy fire. "Holy shit! They are

firing heavy back here!!" Val shouted.
She could hear the screams of the
hostages and locked her sniper rifle. She
fired off shots taking out three men.
Quickly she moved through the house
dodging bullets and taking out several
men on her own. One enemy came up
behind her and put her in a choke hold.
She used her legs and feet to run up the
wall flipping over him pulling him down
and knocking him out.
She did a forward roll on the floor and
pointed her weapon stopping before
pulling the trigger to see Ray staring at
her. "You almost got shot." She said
while standing up.
"I know you wouldn't shoot me." Ray
said confidently.
"Then you don't know me very well..."
Valerie laughed before getting ready to
holster her weapon.
The main target snatched Ray from
behind and held a gun to his head. "Put
down your weapon or I will kill him!!"

he shouted, his voice muzzled under the green mask.

Ray looked into her eyes as he struggled, "Val, just get out here...don't worry about me!"

"I'll do it! I'll kill him! Put down your weapon NOW!" The target shouted. Valerie didn't panic and shot Ray in the leg and the target between the eyes. Ray fell to the ground in pain. "What the hell!" he shouted at her. A large horn sounded showing the end of the training exercise.

Valerie helped him up and he snatched his arm away, "You shot me!"

"It's a flesh wound, and you're alive." Valerie said while holstering her weapon.

Ray grabbed her, "You need to learn that your actions affect other people."

"And you will see one day that so called action saved your damn life! Maybe you need to heal first." She said while glancing at his wound. "He was going to *kill you whether I lowered my weapon or not."*

Ray sighed. Lucas walked in clapping as Valerie walked out of the house. "I like her."

"She is a kamikaze." Ray said while shaking his head.

"No, she is controlled chaos. Passionate and willing to do what is necessary." Lucas said. "She is exactly what I've been looking for…"

Continuing…

As Valerie continued to train and learn from others including Ray, she found her attraction for him grew. He had a mysterious side to him that made her want to get to know him. He was different than any man she had ever met. Val stood in front of Ray sweating. They held eye contact with one another not breaking away. In an instant they created their own language. "What are you thinking?" He asked her.

*"The line we can't cross..." she started.
"But you want to..."*

*"So do you." Val said while breaking
away and walking towards her bag on
the stool. She began ripping the tape off
her hands with her back turned to him.
He walked up behind her, his hands
spreading across her stomach as he
gripped her body and his lips lightly
pressed against the nape of her neck.
Val closed her eyes as she engulfed the
moment having him her weakness, in her
presence.*

*"Tell me..." He whispered.
Valerie turned around and immediately
kissed him wrapping her arms around
his neck. He picked her up and carried
her to the wall as they continued kissing.
The line they could no longer fight. It
was evident that they were more than
willing to cross it.*

*Hours later the two were laying next to
each other in bed at his loft style
apartment with a distant view of the city*

buildings. *"I don't do that often."* Valerie confessed.

"Just with me." Ray laughed.

"I thought you hated me."

Ray shook his head, *"The opposite Val, I fell for you. For some reason with you, I can't fake it like I can with everyone else. So if I don't speak to you, it's because I can't fake it."*

Valerie sat up next to him, looking at him lying in bed shirtless and relaxed. *"You can't?"*

"No, you have this power over me." Ray said while sitting up next to her.

Valerie caressed his face and ran her thumb over his lips. He gazed into her eyes, seeing how they instantly fell in love with each other. He began to ask how he arrived at such a place, and she was wondering how she could break the code. *"Ray..."* she whispered.

Before sharing anymore, their phones lit up in the dark breaking their moment. Ray answered his, *"Hello?"*

"Ray, its Lucas. I need you back at the office, we have a situation." Lucas commented.

"Okay I am on my way."

Lucas on the other end paused he was going to add an additional comment but stopped. "See you soon."

Ray lowered his phone, "I have to go in."

"So do I," Valerie said while looking at text message from her analyst, Casper.

"Ray we can't tell anyone at the office about this. The code…"

Ray nodded, "I know about that as much as you do. I was here before you remember."

The two arrived separately at the office with a critical assignment that immediately had them on a plane to Mexico for a mission regarding the kidnapping of an informant pertinent to a government case. The team didn't ask questions, they just went wherever they were told to go.

After a brutal ambush, bullets firing and killing several hostiles...The two of them plus four others were under siege hustling to get back to the extraction site. "I want you to flag left and take the informant." Ray directed.

"No, you take the informant and I will flag right to misdirect the hostiles." Valerie yelled.

"You never listen!"

Valerie shot a man in the chest yards away as the hostiles were closing the gap. She looked at Ray, "We are out of time! Take him and GO!"

Ray, in dismay and disagreement took the informant to race to the extraction site. Valerie misdirected the hostiles. The concern? Her getting back to the extraction point on time. It was apparent to Ray that Valerie's skills surpassed his own in the field. But worse, she was aware of it.

Ray arrived with the rest of the team and ripped off his vest in anger, "She should've listen to me!"

"Sir, do we wait? Mexican police are in pursuit." The pilot added.

"We can't leave her." Ray answered. After an elongated mission, the team landed safely back in California with the informant. "Great work you two." Lucas said, "You make a great team. You're more alike than you think."

Valerie turned to Ray, "You don't trust me!"

"You don't trust me Val! You're bleeding and you nearly got us all killed."

Valerie stepped back and shook her head, "I did what I did for you and this team."

"No, you have to separate it. When I am here on these missions I am thinking about staying alive, not you."

"Oh that's good, you don't care."

Ray moved closer to her, "It's not that I don't care, I do. I care too much, I just don't show it like you do. You wear it all on your face."

Valerie looked into his eyes as he touched the side of her face. "We will never be. We can't with what we do." Ray whispered.

"How is it so easy for you to turn your back on someone you love. I can't do that to you." Valerie confessed with tears. She was hurt and felt broken inside. He just turned it off like all the words he said to her in private were lies. Ray stopped walking and looked at her, "I never said I was turning my back. I never will either."

Present Day...

The history between Ray and Valerie began at the agency. They connected instantly, but it was the challenge of separating their work from their personal emotions that made things difficult and draining. It spilled into how they worked together. Ray would constantly pull away and Valerie started to give up. Now, Ray, Valerie, and a few agents stood behind a table in the meeting room as Lucas once again explained the current mission. Valerie kept glancing over at Ray, who was now in charge of the team. Casper was right, things had changed since her accident. "We now have a threat on American soil. This mission is crucial and we need to coordinate who is in charge." Lucas stated, "I want the one who is calling the shots...alive."

Valerie looked at Lucas as soon as the words left his lips, "Do you want to reiterate?"

Lucas laughed, "No Val, you just have a tendency to shoot first and not ask any questions."

"It is how I was trained, so train differently and there won't be any problems," Val responded. As the other guys laughed at her snarky comment. Immediately, Val froze in place as her mind recalled a memory of her and Eric when she was working through rehab.

Valerie laid in Eric's arms, the two grew close as she completed her rehab to regain her strength. Eric's fingers touched her healed gun shot wounds, "Did they tell you how you got injured?" He asked already knowing the answer.
"I was out and fell hitting my head." Valerie answered.
"Yea and screw drivers stabbing you in the back..." Eric said without thought. Valerie looked at him, "Yea...how did you know that?"
Quickly, Eric played off her amnesia, "You told me remember?"
"Probably," Valerie commented, "It's all so fuzzy sometimes. I can't really remember."

"Valerie…" Lucas called back breaking her blank stare.

"Ugh yea?" Valerie refocused as she recalled the moment with her husband. Eric knew the entire time, how could she miss that?

"Valerie, are you with us?" Lucas retorted.

"Yea," Valerie got ready to leave the room and stopped Ray, "Can I speak with you?"

"Yea," Ray said as the two of them walked down the hall to a quiet room. "What's going on?"

"Are we good? Because we have a mission here and I want to know that you have my back."

Ray shook his head and folded his arms, "I always have your back Val. It's you that has the problem. Out there on a mission you are reckless when emotions get the best of you. It shows! The whole team wonders if they can rely on you."

"You're kidding right?" Valerie said while squinting her eyes. She fought back anger that emerged from his comments.

"No, why don't you see it! We can't work with you when you get that way. I know I can't, and I won't tolerate that mess anymore."

Valerie shook her head, "Reckless and emotional, that's how you describe me?"

"See no, I am saying when you get like that you are intolerable. Me and the others don't want to be around you. I am sick of it. All this time you never heard from me, that was me spacing away from you…"

"I was out Ray! The last mission I was shot in the back and now I am fighting to remember bits and pieces of my life because someone here wanted me killed!"

"No one here set you up and why would you think that it was me!? If I set you up why would I come to you before anyone else?!" Ray fussed, it annoyed him that she continuously questioned his loyalty. Valerie folded her arms in anger looking at Ray who didn't make eye contact with her. "You're really angry with me…" Valerie retreated her now frustration to cater to his.

"No I'm not, it doesn't phase me anymore." Ray finished.

Valerie shook her head. Why come to her? Why show up if he was going to act like he didn't care about her. "Your words are saying something different than your body language. But what do I know, I am an unreliable emotional reckless agent."

"I never said that, don't put words in my mouth. Point is you need to get your shit together because this mission isn't a joke. The team is relying on you." After saying his words Ray grew quiet and stood against the wall as if he was waiting for her to end the conversation. Valerie shook her head and stopped before opening the door. She turned to face him, "I hear you. I always hear you. Every time we ever argued or you got upset with me I heard you! But since I fell in love with you, you haven't heard me once."

Ray shrugged, "Maybe it's how you're communicating."

"Or maybe you just aren't listening because you're clouded by your frustration."

"If that's what you think," Ray responded.

"You know I never said you were wrong. It is always about you. You who can wound me without ever taking a shot." Valerie said holding back emotion, "By the way, I was shot in the back. So unless you're telling me that it was friendly fire, someone set me up to die and I intend to find out who it was. But you wouldn't know that because you don't listen to me." Valerie finished as she opened the door to see Lucas ready to knock.

"Everything okay?" Lucas asked while looking at the two of them. He overheard some of the commotion.

Valerie looked at Ray and said, "I don't know."

"Well fix it, we have a lot riding on this and I am counting on you two." Lucas demanded. "You aren't enemies as much as you two pretend to be. If you learn to work as partners we can accomplish a whole lot more. But we can't if you guys keep using your weapons to shoot at each other." Lucas noted.

Valerie shook her head, "No shots fired, just one person pistol whipping another." Valerie walked away and left Lucas and Ray in the room alone.

Ray shook his head, "She doesn't understand."

"What is your problem with her?" Lucas asked. He wanted to understand the tension between the two of them, because it was obvious they loved each other.

"I don't have a problem with her, it's how she acts and I can't do it." Ray fussed. "It is emotionally draining."

"Ray you are one of the best agents here. You think five moves ahead before doing anything and you aren't wrong about things. That's your gift and curse." Lucas noted.

"She never stops to ask how her reckless words and actions impact others, that's what I can't tolerate." Ray fussed.

"So what causes it? What causes her to act reckless?" Lucas asked hoping he would get the point.

"I don't know!"

"Maybe that's it, you don't know, you never attempted to find out from her. Maybe it doesn't matter to you, or it does. But no one just acts emotionally for no reason, especially a woman. She is your team mate, find some balance." Lucas said before walking away.

Ray leaned against the wall gathering his thoughts. Things grew draining between him and Valerie. But seeing her, having her back around brought back feelings. The good and the bad. No matter how hard he tried he couldn't share his feelings for her. But, the memories of their secret moments together would creep into his mind. During a struggling time, it was air for him when he felt like he was drowning.

"Are you sleeping on top of the sheets? Ray asked before climbing in bed next to Val.
"Under…" Valerie responded taking a deep breath. "I um, have never slept next to any guy before."

Ray touched her face and set an alarm on his phone, "I guess I will be the first."

"You've been the first for a lot things for me," Valerie added. Within minutes the two fell asleep but not before Val rested her hand on his stomach and she felt him rest his on top of her hand.

#LOVE

Valerie drove to a diner outside of town to see Casper. The two were trying to keep their meetings secret from anyone watching from the agency. She knew going back would mean being watched constantly, but it meant possibly putting Casper in danger. Casper agreeing to help find who was responsible for Valerie's assassination attempt meant she too was now at risk Valerie parked her car and walked inside to see Casper sitting at a booth in the back corner. "Hi!" The waitress greeted them as soon as Valerie sat down. "What can I get you ladies?"

"I'll have diet coke," Valerie responded while taking off her sunglasses.
Casper laughed, "I don't think they will find us out here Val."
"I don't underestimate anyone who was able to shoot me in the back." Val

smirked while responding to her statement.

Casper sipped the ice coffee she ordered, "You and Ray have to travel to Colorado."

"Why?" Val asked. "Can't they send someone else?"

Casper laughed at her response knowing that there was tension between Val and Ray "How about you two just admit you still have feelings and we can get back to saving the country."

Valerie shook her head, "I am married."

"…to a liar who conspired to have you killed." Casper finished, "But hey what do I know."

Valerie cut her eyes at Casper knowing she was right. Casper continued, "You and Ray have to gather intel on the structure of the possible attack in LA. There are two key contacts, Mason and Hadid who run a high investment company we believe is funding this attack."

"Nice." Valerie responded sarcastically while sliding from photo to photo on the tablet, "They're young."

"Now you know why you are going." Casper laughed, then she returned back to seriousness, "They are looking for a consultant and we got you in the door, Ray will play your security." Casper continued, "While you are in the office you have to download their encrypted files so we can target the group who is receiving the funding. This will tell us how deep this goes."

"Now that sounds more like your wheelhouse, can't you hack it?"

Casper shook her head, "No, the type of firewall system they have requires exact copy downloads to infiltrate the data. I physically need the files."

"So you need me to get into their office, assuming that's where they would even keep the information and download it?" Valerie wouldn't accept how simple Casper made it sound.

"Yup, financial records is all we need."

"Great," Valerie looked at her watch, "I need to go and entertain my lying husband who I don't know whether to kill or torture for information."

Casper sighed, "I am so sorry Valerie I know you loved him."

"I am starting to wonder if I did, or if I just loved the idea of him…" Valerie reflected.

"He must stay alive, if he is part of this and it leads back to Lucas, hurting Eric will tip off Lucas."

"Good point," Valerie said while finishing her diet coke, "You just saved his life."

Valerie began walking away and Casper yelled, "We leave at 5:00 am…" she sighed, "good talk."

Valerie went home to meet Eric and Liam for dinner following through with the plan from weeks ago. It was difficult to care considering Val had more information regarding Eric than what she knew before. What was she supposed to do? Continue to act like nothing is wrong? "There she is!" Eric shouted while smiling, "Liam and I were just talking about us all heading to Hawaii one month for vacation."

"Sounds nice." Valerie said calmly. She was fighting to maintain her composure and restrain from grabbing her gun pressed against her skin underneath her shirt.

"Hey sis, thanks for having me over for dinner," Liam said while hugging and kissing her forehead.

"Of course."

"I got some take out and set up the table. I'm sorry I didn't cook babe but I got out the office late today." Eric noted as each of them started fixing their personal plates.

"How are those deals coming along?" Valerie asked now questioning everything about his job.

Eric was stunned by her question, "Um, pretty good just tying up loose ends."

"I know the feeling bro…" Liam started but Val cut him off, "Loose ends huh? I can only imagine. Shocking to learn some things don't work out as planned."

Liam sipped his wine as he felt some tension at the table. Eric chewed his noodles and looked at his wife. Part of him wondered if she knew, but assumed if she did he would be tied to a chair, tortured, and bleeding. "Sometimes they don't and you have to reconfigure the plan."

"That's always a smart idea." Valerie kept staring at him before going back to eating her food.

"Is everything okay?" Liam asked.

"Why wouldn't it be?" The two answered him in unison.

Liam laughed, "forget I asked."

After dinner, Eric went to bed early, sleeping with one eye open while Valerie sat downstairs slowly falling asleep on the couch. She wanted to stay away from him. Remembering what Casper recommended, keeping him alive.

"Are you sure you want to marry me?" Valerie asked Eric as she laid in his arms in their queen size bed.
"Of course," Eric lifted her head to make eye contact with him, "Baby I love you and I can't imagine my life without you. I know we haven't been together long, but who cares."
Valerie sat on her knees and leaned in to kiss him. She felt his hands slide up her back as their kisses grew intense

and he flipped her over to lay on top of her. "I can't wait to make you my wife." Eric whispered. Valerie smiled at him as he kissed her again.

Valerie sat up sweating and looking around the house. Realizing that she was downstairs alone she laid back down and adjusted the gun underneath her pillow. "Are you coming to bed?" Eric asked interrupting the silence. All of this, her life in the suburbs was a coverup for something bigger and she intended to find out what.

"Yea babe."

"Nightmare?" He asked continuing the conversation.

Valerie looked at him standing on the staircase, "No, not this time."

The day of the mission Valerie left before Eric was up and road to the airport base to get on the plane. She grabbed a seat and sipped her coffee as

her sunglasses hid her eyes and thoughts.
Ray looked up from his notes,
"Morning."

"Morning," Valerie lacked emotion as
she was still thinking about Eric.
Casper joined them on the plane and sat
between them, "Great day isn't it!?"

The two of them looked at her, and
shook their heads. "Anyway, I have you
guys set up at a rental house by the lake.
Easy exit if need be."
"You aren't staying with us?" Ray
asked.

Casper shook her head, "No, just in case
the guys ask to come to the house.
Valerie needs to appear to be rich and
alone."

"Except for having a body guard"
Valerie added while looking at Ray. Ray
kept his eye contact with her sharing a

moment before turning his attention back to his notes.

Several hours later they landed in Colorado and rode to the remote house location. As they walked in Ray glanced at Valerie, "I will take the room down the hall, you can have the master."

Casper walked in behind them as Ray walked away. "You guys will get back on track." Casper being a good friend trying to reassure Valerie.

"What do you mean?" Valerie asked while sipping water from her bottle.

"You two share something beyond just missions and guns." Casper responded, "He doesn't see how much it all hurts you." Valerie knew Casper was right. Ray appeared naive to how his actions hurt her.

Valerie winced, "Pain is subjective."

"Not when it comes to this, not you two." Casper said while walking over to the table and tossing a black duffle bag down, "Now, lets talk about what you will use to extract the files. I know you love lip gloss, so here ya go."

"I love this raspberry shade." Valerie detached the bottom to reveal the flash drive, "Clever."

Ray laughed while walking back into the living room, "Not as well as I know you."

"This lip gloss stick is your encrypted flash drive. You will use this to get the information. Ray, the black car out front is what you will drive to escort her to the meeting. Also your wardrobe is laid out in the master. Look sexy, sharp and professional."

"Communications?" Ray asked.

"Yea," Casper held up a small flat micro chip, "this goes right on the flap of skin inside your ear. You can hear us and we can hear you."

"They keep getting smaller."

"Radio check," Ray said to the team while hooking his ear piece around his right ear.
"Mine isn't working…" Valerie said while repeatedly clicking the radio control on and off.
Ray walked up to her and touched her waist while pushing the wired ear piece in all the way. He clicked the radio and it turned on.
Valerie giggled, "My bad."
"I think you did that on purpose so I would touch you."

**"Would you look at that, and you did,"
Valerie winked.**

"Alright, good luck. Oh and your favorite guns are on the table. Good night," Casper said while opening the front door and staring at the two of them before closing it.

For a moment it was slightly awkward the two being alone on a mission again after so much time has passed. "I will make us something to eat," Ray made his way to the kitchen that was stocked with groceries.

"You don't cook." Valerie responded. "You hate it."

Ray laughed, "I never got to cook for you."

"True, but I prefer breakfast. Pancakes if I am being specific."

"I am sure of it" Ray answered while holding a pan.

 "There are certain things I just don't like doing…cooking is one of them," Ray explained, "But I do know how to cook."
Valerie reloaded her weapon, "Okay lets bet, if I hit my target in the center three times you have to make me pancakes."
"That's too easy!" Ray responded with laughter.
"Okay, three times in the same spot."
Valerie was determined, "Are you scared?"
"No, not even close," Ray touched her face and kissed her, "Go ahead, shoot."

"You owe me pancakes anyway," Valerie responded while sitting at the kitchen table watching him mix up the batter.

"I know and I have learn my lesson to not make bets with you."

The tension that was once there disappeared as the two ate pancakes and sat on the couch reminiscing about old times. Instantly, they reconnected and found each other rekindling their feelings. Valerie laughed hysterically and fell back on the couch, "That is not what happened!"

"Yes it is, could you imagine if you were wrong how crazy that would've been!" Ray shouted.
"The agency would've had so much to clean up." Valerie added, "You had to hold me back."
Ray nodded, "I did, not that I ever mind."

Valerie looked at him as they kept eye contact. Ray closed the gap between them on the couch and touched her face as their connection intensified. It was undeniable and hard to ignore when they were alone. He caressed her face with his fingers and she closed her eyes to embrace his touch.

With her eyes closed she felt his lips on hers and wrapped her arms around his neck. He picked her up pulling her body into his. The two got wrapped up in one another before Valerie came up for air. Valerie's breathing grew lighter as she caressed his face. Tempted to go further but doing her best to refrain from doing so. "We should head to bed, we have to get up early."

Ray loosened his grip of her waist as she climbed back on the other side of the couch. "You're right, I'm sorry."

"Hey…" Valerie stopped him and touched his arms, "Don't you ever apologize. I missed kissing you."

Ray smiled, "Really?"

Valerie stood up, "I never lost any feelings. I just learned to live with them."

"Even when you decided to get married?" Ray was curious about her feelings when they went separate ways.

Valerie stopped mid step and sighed, "When I got married it was after my accident. But you made things clear during that last mission in Colombia."

"I did."

Valerie pursed her lips, "We argued and you said we will never be. Period."

"That was a different time Val."

"Yea. I wanted to be with you! I wanted us and then I was shot in the back and got this stupid amnesia memory loss! Now I struggle with what I can remember and when I can remember it!"

Ray paused before speaking, "Funny, you didn't lose memories of us."

"I just wanted to be happy Ray.""

Ray looked at her, "and did you find it?"

Valerie shook her head, "No. Goodnight." She left the room before the conversation could grow any deeper.

Lying in bed Valerie was awake missing Ray though he was just down the hallway.

"What do you love most about the two of us?" Ray asked while holding her in his arms and caressing her back.

"I can be myself around you," Val responded while sipping her drink sitting his lap, "Oh my gosh that's strong."

Ray laughed, "That's what happens when you make the drinks. You have to taste it first."

Valerie smiled, "What about you?"

"You make me happy." Ray said while looking deep into her eyes.

"How did we get here?" Valerie asked herself contemplating how her and Ray arrived at a place of difficulty with one another. Down the hall in the guest bedroom Ray was wide awake thinking deeply about Valerie and the times they had together. "How did we get here?" He asked himself. Each of them could easily blame the other to answer that question.

The next morning Ray was up early dressed and ready to accompany Valerie downtown to the meeting. Valerie fixed her tight black and dark red stripe dress that showed her cleavage. She walked down the hall towards the kitchen area debating about how revealing the dress was. "This is a lot of cleavage," Valerie said to herself before stopping in front of Ray.

Ray stared at her as she stopped and looked back at him. They shared thoughts and he broke the silence, "Were you able to hide your gun in that dress?" Ray cracked a joke to lighten the mood.

Valerie walked by him lightly brushing up against his side, "Absolutely."

Ray checked her out admiring her curves, "Of course you did."

"We should get going driver…" Valerie joked as the two walked out the front door to the car. Ray opened the door and spoke into their communicators located inside their ears, "Leaving the nest."

"Copy." Casper responded while being at a central location with two other analyst.

During the car ride Ray kept glancing in the rear view mirror at Val who looked nervous. It has been a while since being on a mission in the field following her accident. Her hands were shaking as she tried to make a fist and relax.

"Relax, we will be okay. I got your back." Ray commented trying to comfort her.
Valerie smiled at him and winked, "Thank you."
"Doing this mission Valerie we have to trust one another. It's when we don't that it causes unnecessary stress. I don't want that."
"I am aware."

"Good, missions don't need stress."
Valerie sighed feeling badgered, "I got it."

After driving for nearly 30 minutes Ray pulled up to the 15 story office building and parked. They walked towards the entrance of the building as a secretary greeted them both. "Hello, you must be Ms. Brie Anderson." The secretary noted.

"Pleasure to meet you." Valerie said while smiling.
"Is this your body guard?" The secretary asked while looking at Ray, "and your name?"
"Jason," Ray responded while making minimal eye contact.

"Alright well Mason and Hadid are waiting." The secretary guided them to the elevator and they went to the top floor. "Mason has been looking for a consultant for the firm for months now." The secretary said filling the silence.

"Well, hopefully I am what they are looking for."

"I'll say, you're gorgeous." The secretary noticed, "Be careful both of these guys are young and single," she warned.

Ray lightly touched Valerie's back as they stepped off the elevator. The secretary beat them to the main office door and opened it to announce their names to Mason and Hadid.

"Welcome!" Mason said. The secretary was right, Mason was mixed with Spanish and European standing 6'2 with hazel eyes. Hadid was Persian and had a pearly white smile. Immediately both men came off as charismatic.

"You must be Ms. Anderson…" Hadid said while holding out his hand to shake hers.

"Please call me Brie," Valerie suggested, "This is my body guard."

"Oh wow, that important huh?" Mason commented while laughing.

Hadid pushed him, "Please excuse my business partner, lets get started."

Valerie sat down in the leather love seat and neatly crossed her legs in an enticing manner. She immediately captured the attention of both men. "How about you tell me a little more about your business and what you guys are looking for?" Valerie asked.

"We measure success in the stock and financial investment markets." Mason responded, "It started small and now the company is worth $100 million dollars."

"Why do you need a market analysis consultant?" Valerie asked. "Seems like you've got that covered."

Hadid smiled at her and shook his head, "We need a very unique algorithm that not only can measure losses and gains, but stalemates."
"Stalemates?"
"Yea, if the market will maintain over longer periods of time." Mason finished. "We heard you were the best at designing algorithms and have designed something similar to it." Hadid mentioned.
Valerie took a deep breath, "I am."

"Perfect. Can we interest you in a drink Brie?" Mason asked while staring at her legs.

Valerie stood up and walked over to the window to admire the view of the city. "The view is gorgeous."

Hadid jumped up and walked over to her beating Mason out of his chair. "Yes, I actually designed this building."

"With my help of course." Mason commented.

Ray snickered at Valerie's approach and glanced over at the desktop computer a few feet away. He noticed that Valerie left the lip gloss at the crack of the seat for him to see. He quickly grabbed it while they stood talking at the window.

"I would love a tour." Valerie asked while looking at the two of them.

"It would be our pleasure." Hadid answered.

As the three walked to the door Mason stopped, "Does your body guard have to join us?"

Valerie looked at the two of them and smiled, "He can wait here."

"That's fine." Hadid patted Ray on the back, "How about you sit this one out. She doesn't need a bodyguard where we are going."

As they left the room Ray quickly put the flash drive into the computer, "The flash drive is attached."

"Copy, we are accessing the computer now." Casper said while typing quickly on her laptop. "Files are uploading we need at least 3 minutes."

"Take your time," Ray laughed, "Valerie has them wrapped around her finger."

"Sounds like you two are getting along."

Ray nodded, "She is great at what she does."

"I am sure of it."

"Casper, she can also hear everything we are saying." Ray noted.

"Right of course…so sorry!" Casper laughed.

As Ray stood behind the desk waiting for the file load to complete security walked in, "Hey what are you doing?" The guard slid his hand over to his weapon waiting for Ray's response.

"Waiting…I was told to wait for Hadid and Mason to return. They had a meeting." Ray commented while walking towards security. Before the guard could answer Ray swept him into a choke hold putting him to sleep. He dragged his limp body over to the side closet.

"We need to move now!" Ray said harshly under his breath. "Security caught me and he won't be asleep for long."

"Files are finished" Casper said, "Now you guys head to the aircraft base for take off."

As soon as Ray opened the door, the three were standing there. "Someone is in a rush." Hadid commented.

"Ma'am we are late to the airport we must get going."

"Gentlemen, thank you. My office will be in touch as to whether this is a partnership worth pursuing." Valerie said while smiling.

"Ugh okay…thank you." Mason said with suspicion.

Ray lightly touched Valerie's back and guided her to the elevator. "I have a security guard knocked out in the closet," He whispered.

Valerie laughed, "And I am the one with composure issues."

"He started asking too many questions, so we need to go." Ray said as they rode the elevator down to the lobby.

During the drive back to the house Valerie unzipped her dress to change clothes. Ray glanced in the review mirror and saw her sliding out of her dress showing her lace undergarments. He shook his head and laughed, "You were wearing that underneath your dress?"

Valerie winked at him, "Don't be surprised." She slipped into her tight leggings, clipped her weapons belt, and zipped up her black leather jacket.

"I'm not." He whispered to himself trying to keep a clear head.

The two rushed inside the house and began packing up everything. They didn't want to leave a trace of them behind for someone to find. "We need to get to the base now," Ray stressed. He had a feeling the guys were tracking them down.

"Stop!" Valerie said while holding up her hand, "We aren't alone."

"Check the left…" Ray said while pulling his weapon from his holster.

Valerie nodded while walking down the back hallway. Ray walked around to the corner of the front door and killed all the lights. "Valerie can you hear me?" Ray asked over communications.

"Loud and clear," Valerie said in a low tone while holding her gun.

"In 5 minutes we need to be in the jeep driving…understand?"

"Yes," Valerie snuck up behind one of the assailants wearing all black. She grabbed him from behind flipping him over and shooting him once in the chest. "I found one…"

"This is Casper, I will get satellite view and see how many you have." Casper said while typing. She accessed the satellite in their location bring up multiple angles and pictures. "Looks like there are six of them with more headed that way. You guys need to get out now."

Ray was firing off multiple shots hitting two of them, "Copy."

"I am behind the house outside." Valerie said before doing a forward roll and forcefully throwing a hunter's knife into the leg of another assailant. He fell down and she fired two shots in his chest before walking further. "Let's go Ray, I am at the jeep."

"Start driving I am exiting now!" Ray yelled while breathing heavily and shooting at the same time. She started the Jeep, opened the passenger door, and slowly drove off as Ray jumped in.

During the plane ride back to California the two kept looking at each other. It was obvious they were feeling the same thing. "I have no doubt that Mason and Hadid are involved in what is coming."

Valerie said while reloading her weapon.

"You had doubts before?" Ray asked wondering why she would doubt the intel.

"I always have doubts when I am sent on a mission."

"Still don't trust me do you?" Ray laughed under his breath while shaking his head with disappointment.

"It's not you I don't trust." Valerie said while staring back at him. Valerie use to blindly trust the agency and take orders. She never asked questions before the Columbia mission. Ray needed to understand that it wasn't about him. It was about a deeper set up that Valerie was willing to risk everything to uncover.

After landing back in California the two stepped off the plane still holding a disconnect between them. However, Valerie was not going to give up on her plans of finding out who set her up. Lucas walked up to the two of them and stopped, "I am so proud of you two for working well together."

Ray looked at Valerie, "I trust her, she was always a core part of the team."

Valerie nodded, "I have something I have to handle…"

Lucas looked at Ray as she walked away, "Val, what are you about to do?"

"Something I should've done a long time ago." Valerie said while loading her gun and holstering it.

"Keep an eye on her, I believe her memory is coming back and if it does…" Lucas paused while looking at Ray. "Isn't that a good thing?" Ray asked interrupting his thoughts.

"Of course, she is one of our most dangerous operatives." Lucas noted trying to leave out details, "I just want you to stay close. We need it for this mission."

Casper met Ray by the entrance, "Hey did you get it?"

"Here you go. Thank your sidekick over there." Ray joked.

Casper gripped the flash drive and started walking away, but she stopped and retraced her steps to face Ray, "you know if you take some time to listen to her, a lot of the issues you guys have you will uncover are just misunderstandings."

Ray continued to think about Casper's words. "Okay I am off, I know holding lip gloss was awkward!" Casper shouted while running off.

As night fell over California Valerie was done with therapy and done with a fake marriage. She walked inside the house she once called home and absorbed the silence. She walked upstairs and stopped at the doorway staring at her so-called husband, Eric. She raised her gun and pointed it at him. "Pop pop!" Two gun shots.

Eric jumped up looking at his pillow and 2 inches from his ear was a single hole. She hit the same hole twice. She stared at him, "I hope you know I don't miss unless it is on purpose."

"What the hell Val!! What is going on!?" Eric shouted.

"Don't!" Valerie yelled, "You lied to me!"

Eric held up his hands in fear, "No, no, no I never lied to you."

Valerie moved closer to the foot of the bed while pointing the gun, "Do I look like I am person you want to piss off!?"

"No…no," Eric pleaded with tremble in his voice, trying to stay calm.

"You are going to tell me everything. Right now." Valerie said. "Starting with who set me up."

Eric sighed, "Can you lower the gun?"

Valerie laughed, "That was a stupid question." She tighten her grip on the handle, finger was trigger ready. "You're going to tell me what I want to know or the next bullet goes between your eyes."

"My business was falling behind and catching tons of debt. I needed money and I was approached with an offer that would pay me 5 million dollars."

"What was the offer?"

"It was a deal down in Colombia I needed help with," Eric started, "Afterwards I was approached and offered an additional 3 million…to marry you."
Valerie squinted her eyes, "This was all planned!?"

"I did…I did fall in love with you Val. The love I felt was real," Eric explained.

"I will kill you! Stop with the add ons and finish the story." Valerie demanded. She started to feel tears run down her cheeks. It was hard for her to stay impartial, emotion was taking over.

"In Columbia there was a deal going down that I needed and Lucas offered to send his team in to handle it if he received a cut of the pay and if…" Eric paused, "If you were a casualty."

"Lucas…" Valerie whispered, "Why would he set me up?"

"I don't know Valerie, but I agreed. I needed the money before things tanked. I needed it to save the family business."

"Let me get this straight, you love me but were willing to kill me for money?" Valerie asked while tilting the gun, "Does that sound right? Say it back."

Eric shook his head as he climbed out of bed and stood up, "It sounds crazy but I am telling you…"

"You aren't telling me shit!" Valerie shouted, "You and Lucas set me up."

"Valerie it wasn't personal. I don't know why Lucas needed you gone but it was part of the deal! When that failed, I was told to connect with you and marry you."

"You have 30 seconds to leave and never come back. If I ever see you again Eric I will kill you and bury you in the deepest ditch I can find." Valerie threatened.

"Val…" Eric started.

"Leave!!!" Valerie yelled while lowering her gun. But before Eric could reach the door Valerie said one more thing. "You knew I was a trained operative this entire time?"

Eric nodded, "I did. That's why I was afraid to betray you."

Valerie laughed, "Obviously not scared enough. Sign these…" Valerie said while handing him divorce papers.

Eric took the pen and immediately signed divorce papers and ran down the stairs in fear. He got down to his car as it was in the middle of the night. His car exploded before he could reach the end of the block. Valerie heard the noise and ran downstairs out the door to the middle of the street to see the glowing flames and cloud of smoke. It was only a few seconds before neighbors came out of their homes and 911 emergency was flooded with calls.

Valerie stood in the street looking at her neighbors panic and scream. She was frozen and didn't react at all. Part of her was sad but the feelings disappeared as she remembered all of this was fake. Her entire life after her accident was a lie. The memories of her real profession filled her brain as she whispered, "I remember."

She walked back inside to see Ray sitting on one of the stools at the island kitchen counter. "You okay?" He asked. He had a surprising way of showing up unexpectedly.

"I hope you aren't responsible for that." Referencing the explosion in the street. She walked over to grab the phone and dial 911.

"No. I did not." Ray said, "I came here because I was worried you were going to kill him."

"I was," Valerie retorted.

"911 what is your emergency?"

"Oh my gosh there is a huge explosion in the street! Please send help! I think that was my husband!!" Valerie cried and yelled acting out in fear and tears. "We are sending emergency services now."

Valerie hung up and looked at Ray, "He was part of this Ray."

"With Lucas?" Ray asked in shock.

"Yes, how did you know?"

Ray recalled his conversation with Lucas, "Lucas was um worried about how much you remember. He made a comment and it threw me off."

"I do remember, and I know that mission was Lucas's idea. He was adamant about sending me. I don't know why he wanted to kill me."

"I don't either, but we have a bigger problem. Your brother is knee deep in a possible attack on this city and has no idea." Ray noted.

Valerie leaned against the wall, "I have to protect him."

"Hey…" Ray said while moving close to her and touching her face, "I will help you."

"I don't know how much longer I can resist you." Valerie whispered while staring at his lips. She caressed his arms and touched his neck.

"Then don't anymore," Ray whispered while leaning in to kiss her.

Suddenly there was a knock at the door, "Hello! This is the county police!"

"I should go." Ray said while pulling back. Valerie watched him leave and then made her way to the door. She stood still as multiple police officers stood on her porch.

#FAMILY

The following morning was the first time in a years Valerie woke up in bed alone. She walked to the bathroom, not having been afraid from a nightmare but feeling revengeful. She made her way down the stairs and saw Ray drinking hot tea at the counter.

"Are you keeping tabs on me again?" Valerie asked while grabbing a mug from the cabinet.

"No. I didn't want to wake you because you were sleeping peacefully. I figured that was the first time in a while."

Valerie started the coffee maker and sat down across from him, "It was."

"What did the police ask you last night?" Ray inquired while sipping herbal tea he found in the cabinet. He was always a tea drinker but Valerie began drinking tea during their time together.

"There was no body. I have no idea what happened to Eric." Valerie said with confusion in her voice, "I don't know if he was kidnapped, disappeared, or was afraid and ran."

"How about all of the above." Ray noted, "He isn't the problem anymore, this bomb threat is and we have to find a way to help Liam."

"Well, where is Casper?" Valerie asked.

"I am right here, just had to grab my computer from the car." Casper said while standing at the kitchen entrance with her tech gear. She raised the laptop, "Shall we get started?"

Valerie froze in shock at the two entering her home without notice or permission, "Did all of you decide to enter my house while I was sleeping?"

"Yes" they responded in unison.

Valerie sighed in annoyance, "I carry a weapon so you guys should know better."

Ray laughed, "I do know how dangerous you are. I also know that your brother is in danger and we have coordinated a plan to stop the bomb threat before it is too late. Are you in?"

"Of course, fill me in." Val responded.

"Okay," Casper began typing on her computer, "your brother has a meeting with Dale Asahari who is the rumored leader of this plot."
"Have we confirmed this intel?" Valerie asked.

"The source is reliable," Casper answered.

Val looked at the computer with pictures of the known threats, "He doesn't know he is walking into a trap."

"Because of the information you gathered I was able to uncover the buyers for the pieces they needed to activate their bomb and schematics to steal the money from the treasury." Casper continued.

Valerie was getting flustered, "How can I help my brother!"

Ray massaged her shoulders as he often did to help her relax...

"Relax, when you are relaxed you can hit your target." Ray whispered in her ear.

"You are making it hard to relax." Val smiled while slightly turning her head towards him.

Ray lifted his hands off her shoulders and step back. "You have to penetrate your brother's office, that way you have a reason to be there."

Casper began typing "that's a good idea. I can make credentials for you that's related to the job he thinks you have."

Valerie sighed, "I hope I can get him to understand."

Ray knew about the disconnect between her and her brother Liam for years.

"Do you have a family?" Ray asked as the two laid in back with the moonlight peeking through the curtains.
Valerie lifted her head off the pillow, messy from being deeply intimate with

him, "I do, but I thought we aren't supposed to talk about our families?" Ray sat up, shirtless and caressed her back, "we aren't but I just have this urge to get to know you."

Valerie nodded in agreement, "tell me about your family and I will tell you about mine."

"I have a sister." Ray started

"I have a brother. We don't speak much but he is my only sibling."

"Don't speak much?"

"Yea" Valerie said while reflecting on her relationship with her brother. She lifted her cell phone, "he doesn't call me anymore."

Ray looked at Valerie showing sincere concern for her brother being mixed up in her true job. "I asked for this life, not him. So he shouldn't die because of it." Valerie said while getting up and walking towards the stairs, "set it up."

"She is feisty in the morning," Casper joked while typing on her computer. Ray followed her upstairs and knocked on the door as Valerie was beginning to change clothes. Valerie laughed, "Now you knock."

"You made such a big deal earlier about not knocking."

"Ray how do I protect my brother in all of this and still find out who tried to kill me?" Valerie found herself overwhelmed with trying to do it all without help. Throughout getting parts of her memory back she was frustrated with the juggling of who to trust and who not to trust. She walked over to towards Ray and pushed the door shut, "I want to show you something," she said in a soft voice while taking off her t-shirt to reveal her back.

Ray looked down and saw the healed gun shot wounds. He ran his finger tips across her back and saw her muscles expand and digress from her breathing slowly. Valerie turned around covering her upper body with her arms, "Every other wound on my body I made a choice to get. But these two…someone else tried to make that choice for me."

"I'm sorry I wasn't there to protect you."

Valerie shook her head as tears fell from her eyes, "My husband betrayed me Ray."

"I wouldn't Val. If you can trust anyone…" Ray started speaking positively in hopes she would let her guard down, "Do you trust me?"

Valerie looked into his eyes and he saw her vulnerability, he saw her pain. "Yes" she whispered while leaning her head against his chest. He lifted her head and kissed her as she tighten her arms around his neck. Ray picked her up, she wrapped her legs around his waist, "Hold onto me," he whispered.

He carried her over to the bed and laid her down with him lying on top. For a second he stopped and looked into her eyes, Valerie pulled his shirt, and he slide it above his head revealing his muscular upper body.

The two stopped and stared at each other. Just taking a moment to reconnect. The anger, the pain, the emotions took a toll on them. But, now while lying in her arms he had his moment to remember the Valerie he loved so much. The woman he fell in love with. "What?" Valerie smiled while touching his face. His eyes were shut.

"Shh...lets stay like this." He said while absorbing the moment.

"I am not going anywhere" Valerie said while kissing his lips.

"You know you aren't as crazy as people try to make you seem." Lucas commented while staring at Valerie sit across from him at his desk.
"Crazy?"
"Yes. Emotionally unstable…" Lucas noted.
"Who are these people?" Valerie asked wondering who was saying things about her on the team. "I have been on countless missions with these people." Lucas sat up in his chair, "Val, you are one of the best operatives we have on the team. These agents put themselves in your hands every mission. If I thought for a second you were crazy, you wouldn't be here."

Valerie stood up ready to leave the room when Lucas spilled one more thing, "But Ray seems to think otherwise..."

Valerie jumped up in the middle of the night to see Ray sleeping next to her. He laid there peacefully resting and she woke up sweaty again from another memory. She creeped downstairs to the kitchen for some water and sat down contemplating her dream. Fighting to remember the entire dream. She wanted to know if Ray had a role in any of this. "Come on Valerie..." she whispered to herself.

"Do you think I am some emotional case?!" Valerie fussed pushing Ray to the side confronting him.
"I already told you what I think of you." Ray responded, "And I told you to do something about it."

"Do me a favor Ray, next time you want to throw a stone at me evaluate yourself first." Valerie walked off as she left Ray standing in the hallway after leaving Lucas's office. Ray glanced across the hall to see Lucas's name on the door.

"Our secret is what damaged it all." Valerie said to herself out loud. She shook her head as the memories flooded her mind between her and Ray.

Ray caressed her hair as she laid in bed barely covered by the bed sheets. He stared at her thinking she was asleep but she was awake with her eyes shut. "I probably shouldn't say this, but I am in love with you Valerie and I have only ever said that to one other person."

He got up and walked to the bathroom as Valerie slowly opened her eyes. Not knowing what to say or what to think. Ray was the first man to ever tell her that he loved her. A part of her smiled at the thought that he was vulnerable with his feelings.

However, for Valerie it was back and forth in her mind. It was backlash and arguing then faithful words and love. She didn't know what to believe about the man she shared her bed with. He said trust him, but could she?

"You are up in the middle of the night, what's wrong?" Ray asked breaking her spur of thoughts.

"You scared me."

"No I didn't, you probably have a gun in your lap," Ray responded.

Valerie nodded and laughed as she placed a gun on the counter from her lap.

"So what is bothering you?" Ray continued.

"I am having trouble knowing what and who to believe."

"About?"

"You and I."

"You're questioning me and you?" Ray asked while slightly squinting his eyes at her, "Why would you do that?"

"There are things I am having trouble accepting. But that's not something that needs a discussion."

"If it is bothering you…"

"No, everything you ever said about me was true." Part of Valerie became comfortable with accepting whatever people said about her. Didn't matter if it was actually true or not. She realized people have stopped listening to anything she had to say.

Ray was confused by her comment as he was at times when she choose to be vague and critical. But a piece of him knew what it was about. He didn't know how to respond or whether he even wanted to respond. Majority of the time he refrained from responding as a way to push her to say what was really on her mind. As a result, the two would disagree and end up arguing. It was a tactic that didn't work very often but still he does it.

"I am going back to bed." She said while walking away to head back upstairs. "You can join me if you want."

Ray stared at her taking each step before deciding to join her. He knew eventually the two would have more to discuss. Their ability to hide their feelings good or bad from one another was something that damaged their ability to work well together. It also made it difficult for them to be around each other.

Valerie wanted to make sure everything was in place not only to protect innocent people but also her own family. Liam was her priority and she didn't want anything to happen to him. Valerie was tirelessly practicing and working on strengthening her memory. Certain things in her past was cloudy and difficult to connect the dots to certain missions that held some importance. Her relationship with Ray was the first memory she had. It was the one connection that appeared clear in her mind despite the back and forth of trust. Her memory made sure she remembered their secret moments together.

Valerie pulled up to a loft building in a newly developed back portion of town. She got out of her car and took the elevator up to a studio style apartment with a view of the bay and shipyard imports. Casper turned around and smiled at her friend, "What do you think?"

"Of what?" Valerie asked while walking towards the center of the room. "What is this place and why did you have me come here?"

"Wow…you don't remember do you?"

Valerie tapped the side of her head, "I hit my head and it kind of knocked out some of my memory…"

Casper smiled, "Of course smart ass. You purchased this place. This was your back up location hide away. No one at the agency knows about it except me."

"I purchased this place?"

"Yup" Casper handed her the keys, "I figured you wouldn't want to stay in the house that was once for you and Eric."

"I can't really sleep there." Valerie said while noticing the eclectic style of the loft and earth tone color design. Everything looked hand picked for a purpose from the wall panels to the table. She took a minute to try and remember ever purchasing the place.

"I dd something!" Valerie said while sitting down next to her friend as she typed rapidly on the computer.
"Okay I will bite, what did you do?"
"I purchased a loft." Valerie smiled, "I needed a spot that is off the grid and this one is perfect." Casper reached for the keys and Valerie pulled her hand

back, "you are the only person that knows about it."

"Ooo that means I know something that Ray doesn't know!"

Valerie squinted her eyes at Casper while standing up behind her, "Ray?"

"Yes, I know about you two" Casper said while rotating her chair to face Valerie and return eye contact. "You can hide things from everyone else, but I have eyes all over."

"Not unless you bugged my phone." Valerie joked. However, Casper kept a straight face. "Seriously Casper!?"

Casper laughed, "No, I didn't bug your phone. I see how he looks at you in meetings and how he responds to you. I know…"

Valerie took a deep breath, "Just don't tell anyone, here is an extra set of keys…"

"Why are you giving me these?" Casper asked while looking down at the three gold keys.

*"**Because if anything ever happens to me here I need to know someone is aware of my back up plan.**"*

Valerie walked towards Casper, "That's when you revealed you knew about me and Ray."

"Yes. You two could hide certain things but not your feelings for one another."

Valerie nodded, and walked over to a vacant wall. She lightly touched the wood and pressed against it making a compartment pop out revealing weapons, flash drives, money, passports, and identifications. She turned and looked at Casper, "Looks like I was ready for anything."

Casper took a deep breath while thinking about how much she knew about her friend, "Val if you want to know who you are, I can help."

"How?" Valerie asked while pushing the compartment back into the wall.

"Silly girl, I have been your analyst on every mission you have been on since we joined the agency. I was assigned to you in the very beginning."

Valerie walked into the kitchen, grabbed two wine glasses and a bottle of wine from the fridge, "I guess we are in for the night."

Two hours later the two were sitting on the floor laughing and reminiscing. "You graduated top of your class with scores that surpassed Ray's." Casper commented.

"I was better than him?"

Casper laughed, "Are you kidding me, you were and still are. Didn't stop him from falling in love with you." Valerie lowered her head thinking about Casper's comment. "You two are more alike than you realize," Casper continued.

Valerie lowered the wine glass from her lips and looked at Casper who withdrew some emotion from her statement. It grew silent between the two of them, almost an awkward silence. Valerie took a deep breath, "I still love him."

"I know, that's why you two argue so much." Casper noted, "Doesn't make sense to me though."

Valerie got up and walked over to look at the view of the bay, "Casper tomorrow I have to go in and try to find out what the plan is. I can't worry about why Ray and I argue."

"No…no" Casper started, "You two just need to agree to either be together or separate forever. Lives now depend on it."

Valerie nodded, "We have to make a choice."

"Exactly, or innocent people could end up collateral damage and not on purpose."

Liam was the current city manager handling all city wide projects and funding. That meant the project on the corner of the city hall building and treasury office was his baby; his project. The two men drafted to contract the building for the development were planning on robbing the treasury building. The following morning a meeting was set with those two men. Liam was standing outside of the city hall building when he noticed a black convertible parked by the curb.

Out stepped his sister Valerie in a tight low cut wine colored dress and 5 inch black heels. She grabbed her black bag and walked up to them as they stood shocked staring at her. Valerie was known for using sex appeal to attract the attention of her male targets and it worked. Liam cleared his throat, "Valerie…" He was caught of guard to see her join the project as his liaison, "I had no idea you were assigned to this project."

"I was just informed about it myself…" Valerie said while taking off her sunglasses and smiling at the two men, "Pleasure to meet you two."

Liam took a deep breath, "This is Valerie and she will be the liaison between us and the treasury building and making sure that both portions of the building plan go smoothly. Alright lets walk over to where we have already broke ground on the new building."

They walked together two blocks to a sectioned off lot that had nearly one hundred construction workers and a building that was nearly finished. "I see your construction team has done an amazing job with staying on schedule for everything." Liam said while looking around.

Valerie looked around trying to learn the exits and entrances of the area. Casper was back at headquarters listening and using city cams to get a visual. Lucas walked inside, "How is she doing?"

"Like her normal self." Casper responded.

"Really?"

Casper laughed, "No."

"You have a unique sense of humor Casper."

"I like to think so sir." Casper responded. As Lucas was walking away Casper's phone buzzed with an alert. She lifted her phone to see a message and her eyes widen shocked by the information. Immediately, she turned her phone downward while glancing around the room.

"As you can see gentleman this building will have 14 floors and be one of the largest buildings in the area." Liam explained as they walked through the area. "I will stop here because we are still finalizing construction."

"It sounds good. What do you think ma'am?" One of the men asked.

Valerie guided her attention back to the men in front of her, "I think it is an expensive project for just one building."

The men laughed and nodded as Liam cut his eyes at his sister. The men walked ahead of her and Liam grabbed her arm, "Can you try not to ruin this for me?" He whispered harshly under his breath.

Valerie snatched her arm away from her brother, "Ruin what brother? I am here to provide support."

"Are you sure that is all you are doing?"

Valerie looked at her brother and paused before answering. They were on good terms since their dinner together trying to smooth things over. However, Valerie never intended for her job to intertwine with her family. This meant lying to the people she had to protect, "Yes, that is all I am doing."

"Good, because I don't want any problems Valerie. I mean it." As her brother walked away she took a deep breath. Casper chimed in over the comms, "I hope he wasn't serious about having no problems."

Valerie laughed, "Unfortunately, he is dead serious."

The group continued to view the site and the men kept answering messages on their phone. "Valerie can you get close enough to use the transmit to steal and make a duplicate copy of that guys phone?"Casper asked speaking into her head set.

"Yes" Valerie whispered. As they began making their way back to the city hall building Valerie tripped and fell on one of the men swiping his phone from his jacket pocket. "Oh my gosh I am so sorry!" Valerie laughed at herself, "it's these heels, maybe they are too high."

The man held onto her arms, "Of course, I was just glad I was here to catch you."

"Me too" Valerie responded as she quickly used the transmitter to make a copy of the phone.

Liam rolled his eyes at his sister's clumsy antics, "Forgive her wearing heels isn't a forte for her." Valerie held onto the man a few extra seconds to put the phone back in his pocket.

"Relax," Valerie whispered to her brother. She left the meeting and walked to her car. "Casper did you get anything?"

Casper, who left the agency, was sitting at Valerie's loft typing on her machine, "yea and you're going to want to see this. Hurry back."

Valerie started the ignition for her car and looked at her brother still talking to the two men. One man glanced over and saw her staring at them. He squinted his eyes and Valerie knew they recognized her. "Valerie! Valerie!" Casper yelled.

"Yea?"

"Are you on your way back? Ray is looking for you."

"He can keep looking. I was made so we need to move quickly."

"You're rusty" Casper joked.

"Apparently, or maybe I did that on purpose," Valerie laughed. She drove to her loft outside the city and stepped off the elevator into the living room space to see Casper and Ray. "Good to know Ray you have found this place."

"I need to talk to you now" Ray said while pulling her into the kitchen space. "I discovered something about the contractors involved in this development..."

"What?"

"Maurice Santos..." Ray said slowly. Valerie stared at him as her memory didn't recognize the name.

"I don't recognize that..." Ray held up his phone displaying a picture of his face, "Do you remember now?" He asked.

Valerie stood on the balcony staring at her target. He looked back at her, not shocked, nor surprised. Within seconds...two shots.

"Columbia..." She whispered, "He was the last face I remember before I was shot!"

"Valerie, his name is attached to the contracting company that is part of the development."

"Why? Why is he back!?"

Casper interrupted, "I can answer that! I looked at the logs from that mission and found that $3 million dollars was stolen from Santos. However, we never logged any cash collected."

"Ray...do you remember finding any cash on site?" Valerie asked.

"No, once you were shot we got out of there."

"So if I have this right, someone within the agency stole $3 million dollars from Santos who is linked to Columbia drug smuggling?"

"Bingo!" Casper shouted.

"I knew one of the men recognized me! My brother…he called me sister. I have to get back to him or he'll be in danger." Valerie pleaded.

"I have hacked into his phone. He will be back on the site in an hour." Casper said.

"I am going to get him!" Valerie said while slipping off her heels and opening her arsenal of weapons.

"Valerie you can't go in alone." Ray said as he watched her get ready.

"Then join me, but either way I am going back."

"Yes! The gang is back together! This is more like it!" Casper shouted with excitement. Valerie and Ray looked at her. "What? I am just happy that's all."

Valerie tossed Ray a nine millimeter pistol. Ray shook his head, "I will take oversight watch, so I need something stronger and bigger than this."

Valerie smirked, "No problem."

Valerie knew that her brother was in danger. Not knowing if Santos was involved in her set up or if it was just an inside job made her more afraid of losing her family. She tried to not let the emotions show on her face and do what Ray always told her to do; focus on the mission.

"Do you still hate me?" Liam asked as he sat next to her in the hospital bed. Valerie was heavily medicated after her surgery and in and out of consciousness.

Valerie slowly shifted her body trying to become comfortable. It was obvious she was groggy from the meds but she attempted to answer her brother, "I don't hate you. You just leave me behind."

Liam touched her hand, "I would never leave you behind. You are my only sister."

"Thank you."

Valerie loaded her weapon and navigated the building site trying to stay hidden. "Can you hear me Val?" Ray asked while looking at her through the sniper rifle scope.
"I can, can you see me?"
"Yes."

"Good, glad to know you have my back up there..." Valerie said in a soft voice while coming upon a group of men speaking. She watched as she saw one of the men was her brother. "I found Liam."

"Yea I got them. Be advised there is a black SUV near that tractor that has one man inside."
"Copy"
"Liam, we have every intention of upholding our end of the deal, but we need the additional $1 million we discussed." One man commented. Valerie snapped a picture and sent it to Casper.

"Casper I am sending you a photo right now."

Casper who was back at the loft pulled up the photo and began facial recognition. "Got it. That man is assumed to be Santos right hand. Marquez is his name. He is ex Columbian special forces."

"That is the man that recognized me." Valerie responded.

"Valerie, these men are ex military special forces, they know what they are doing." Casper responded, "You need to be careful."

"I will get you your $1 million!" Liam shouted, "There is no need to get aggressive."

"Valerie, they pulled a weapon on him." Ray responded. "I can take out two if you have a plan to get him out of there."

Valerie looked at the yellow tractor a few feet away from her, "I have a plan. Be ready to go." Valerie ran over to the tractor, climbed inside, found the keys on the dash board and bulldozed through the pile of wood towards the group. Immediately gun shots were firing at the machine as a few of the men pulled out their weapons as they retreated.

Valerie jumped off the tractor and took cover. Overwatch, Ray took out two of the men. "Valerie one of them is chasing after Liam, they entered the building structure on the east side."

"Got it!" Valerie yelled as she took off running. Chasing after the man that was threatening to kill her brother. Liam turned the corner and tried to find somewhere to hide. The man kept his finger on the trigger tip toeing around the open area looking for Liam.

Valerie fired off one shot hitting the guy in the arm as she walked up to punch him in the face. The guy dropped his weapon and swung back hitting

Valerie in the face. The guy quickly locked her in a chock hold as she struggled to break free. Valerie grabbed his wrist and he began punching her in her right side. "I am more than happy to finish what they started," he whispered while chocking the life out of her. She stomped on his foot, swung her head back hitting him in the face.

The guy swung back and she caught his arm breaking his wrist. "Ahhhhh!!!!" He yelled. Liam poked his head out from around the corner and watched his sister fighting the guy. "Valerie!" He yelled in fear she would get hurt.

"Liam get down!" Valerie said while flipping the guy over and wrapping her thighs around his neck. She pulled his arm and snapped his neck. She slowly crawled away from the dead body and spit out some blood onto to the concrete.

Liam ran over to help his sister and held her, "Are you okay?"

"Yea...I am fine... you ok?"

"Yea, yea...so do you mind telling me how you were able to shoot that guy from way over there in the arm?" Liam asked. "In addition to kicking his ass like that?"

Valerie coughed, "I think that we have a lot to talk about."

"Yea, lets get out of here." Liam said while picking her up.

"So that's it you're just going into the military?" Liam asked as he watched his younger sister pack a suitcase to leave.
"Just because you know what you want to do with your life doesn't mean that I

know what to do with mine!?" Valerie yelled.

Liam sighed, "It's dangerous out there! You could....you could die!"

Valerie walked over to her brother, "I will be okay..."

Liam hugged his sister and held her tight, "I don't want anything to happen to you."

"I know...nothing will. Promise."

#IREMEMBER

Valerie woke up gasping for air while lying in an ice bath in her loft apartment. She looked over to see Ray sitting on the counter, "Glad to see you're awake. That guy gave you a beating."
"Where is my brother?" Valerie asked while climbing out of the tub and covering her naked body.

"He is in the living room with Casper." Ray paused before releasing his thoughts, "Val…"

"What?" Valerie was shivering as her skin was slightly pale from soaking in ice.

"He has questions; I figured you would want to answer."

Valerie knew that killing that guy and showcasing any skills in that arena would cause her brother to ask questions. She shook her head, angry that she would have to be honest with him because lying was no longer something she wanted to do. "I'll answer them," she whispered.

Ray grabbed her by the waist before she could walk out of the bathroom, "opening that door means putting him in harms way."

"He is already in danger because he is my brother. Knowing will help me protect him." Valerie confessed, "He is my brother."

Ray let her go so she could walk out. He watched her and sensed her need to protect her family. It was something he always knew about her.

Ray continued to touch her face as she went on talking about her mother and father. "You said you and your brother are at odds…"

Valerie sat up wrapping the sheets around her body and looking down at him as he rested his head on the pillow. "Just because me and my brother are at odds doesn't mean I won't protect him."

Ray lightly touched her back, "I know you will, but telling him the truth about who you are and what you do means putting him in danger Val."

Valerie turned her attention back to the view outside the window with the moonlight reflecting off the white sheets, "I know."

Valerie found some clothes and joined Casper and Liam in the living room. "Oh good you are alive! I was worried! Are you okay? Who was that guy? How were you able to shoot him from where you were?"

Casper's eyes widen as she heard the out pour of questions from Liam. Valerie cleared her throat and said, "Casper can you give me and my brother a moment."

"Sure, I was thirsty anyway."

"Liam...I am not in the military..."

"Wait...what? You're not in the military?" Liam was confused, "but I watched you pack and leave."

"I was recruited into a special government agency and was trained as a special operative." Valerie confessed to her brother. She watched his eyes transition from confusion to fear.

"Operative?"

Valerie nodded, "Yes. I never was a city employee. Unbeknownst to me, that was a cover up."

"What the hell Val…!" Liam threw his hands up and shook his head.

"Listen to me! I will protect you I know these men know who you are!"

Liam snatched his hand back, "You know them! The men who tried to kill me!? Valerie I nearly died because of your mission or whatever the hell this is!"

"Liam…"

He jumped up angry from being lied to for several years, "What about the letters you sent home to mom!? Were those lies?! You were never in those places!?" Valerie paused as she tried to answer her brother's questions, "Liam…"

Liam cut her off, "So who are you?" He looked into her eyes and Valerie could see the hurt and pain. He was afraid but deep down he knew he needed answers despite his anger towards her.

Valerie touched his shoulder, "I am your sister. I always have been and always will be."

"…and she saved your life." Ray interrupted while standing by the couch. Liam turned his head towards him and frowned. "I remember you. You were at the hospital."

"Yes I was. I work with your sister and have for years." Ray explained.

"So the accident that put you in the hospital…?" Liam asked, "Was that a real thing?"

"Yes, I was set up. On my last mission I was shot twice in the back." Valerie answered, "I am back to figure that out Liam." Liam pursed his lips withholding any more feelings. Valerie looked at Ray who shrugged his shoulders. Ray didn't want Liam to know anything, however, desperate times opened that door.

"Liam," Ray started, "We are here to help you. So why don't you start by telling us how you met those men and what they want with $1 million dollars."

"I made tea!" Casper said while sitting two mugs down on the coffee table.

Liam cleared his throat, "They reached out to me with interest in bringing their business to the area. They heard about the new office building structure and wanted to be involved."

"Did your office do any research?"

Liam shook his head, "No, staff is light in the office and we are on a tight budget. Much of the city's money was invested into this project with hopes of bringing in more funds over the next six years."

Casper sighed, "So how is Santos going to rob the treasury and blow up half the city?"

"It is called revenge Casper," Valerie answered.

"I knew something was strange about these guys! How could I be so stupid!"

"Liam don't blame yourself. They found you because of me."

"I need to get home." Liam was ready to leave and be alone with his thoughts.

Valerie quickly looked at Ray and shook her head no.

"Look man, these guys know who you are, so how about I go with you." Ray offered to give Valerie peace of mind.

"Whatever, I will see you tomorrow Val. Hopefully some sleep will give me some ease." Liam said slowly walking out the door towards the elevator with Ray. Valerie rushed behind them and Ray stopped her, "I will protect him Valerie…promise."

Valerie nodded, "Thank you."

"Of course," he kissed her forehead and joined Liam in the elevator.

Valerie walked back into the loft and sighed in grief, "This is a mess Casper."

"Yes, but I have some information I am sure you are going to want."

"Continue…"

"Lucas was behind your shooting. The bullets pulled from your back were from one of the agency's registered rifles," Casper explained. "That month there were several phones calls between him and these phone numbers." Casper turned the computer towards Valerie so she could review the numbers for herself.

"How did you get this? Seems like Lucas would cover his tracks."

Casper nodded, "He did, but I am good. When they delete things off the drive in our agency it is stored on the server for a period of time."

Valerie glanced at Casper with a shocked look. Casper continued, "Valerie…I designed the system."

"Lucky for me," Valerie smiled. "So whose number is this?"

"One is registered to a burner phone I can't crack. However, these three…one is Eric's phone, Jason's phone…." She stopped and looked at her friend, hesitant to say who the last number belonged to.

"and the third?" Valerie asked.

"It's Ray's phone Val."

Valerie leaned back, "So you're saying that either Jason or Ray shot me?"

"I thought Ray was on the ground with you on that mission? How did he reach the house and shoot a long range shot?" Casper asked.

"Fine. If he didn't shoot me, then this is saying he possibly knew about it!"

"Alright, so we just got the band back together. Lets not jump to any conclusions!" Casper pleaded to Valerie trying to keep her from reacting instead of thinking.

"Casper..." Valerie said while getting up from the couch, "Ever since my memory has started coming back I don't know who to trust! Not the surgeon, the therapist! Not even my damn husband!!"

"Ex husband...we saw to that." Casper corrected while pointing at her.

"I don't care. You and Ray are all I have left and now this is telling me he is possibly more involved that I wanted to believe."

"Val, we don't know what Ray knows. But maybe you should start with trying to remember the days leading up to the mission." Casper sighed while shrugging her shoulders, "Maybe start with drinking some tea and going to sleep. That's how it all started right? Nightmares?"

"Yea"

"Then go back to sleep and trust your mind to want to remember."

Meanwhile, Ray was guarding the windows and laying out extra weapons to help keep Liam safe. Liam walked to his refrigerator and opened a bottle of beer, "You want one?"

"No thanks" Ray answered.

Liam cleared his throat, "You were the one who told me about what happened to my sister."

"I was."

"You also lied to me," Liam responded while sipping his beer.

"I did what I had to do to protect your sister and the mission."

Liam stared at Ray as they were speaking and he sat down on the couch, "You love her…"

Ray took a deep breath, "This isn't a good time to discuss any of this Liam. You have been through a lot including risk getting shot."

Liam laughed, "Don't try to play the post traumatic stress card with me. I am fine and I know what I saw. You kissed her in the hall way."

"Your sister and I have history. That's all."

Liam walked over to him as he stood by the window, "If I am right and you are in love with her. That means she was nearly killed on your watch by someone you both trust."

Ray looked into his eyes as the two stood off fighting back any words that would cause an argument. "I am not going to explain my actions to you."

"You don't have to. Your actions speak for themselves. Have a good night." Liam said while walking away towards the room down the hall. "Have a drink, you need one."

"How long before we reach the US border?" Ray shouted.

"At least 20 minutes," the pilot responded.

"Shit! Hurry up!!" Ray was panicking and fearful he would lose her. "Come on Val stay with me...come on honey."

Valerie slowly opened her eyes, "Hey..."

"Hey there..."

"What's happening? Where...whe..." Valerie was in and out of consciousness.

"Hey! Hey honey stay with me. Come on remember when we ran away together and spent all day on the beach in Cabo? We were um locked away in the room and drunk wine and ate food..." He shared the story while rocking her in his arms.

Valerie started coughing, "I...yea..."

"I told you that night I was falling in love with you," Ray shared, "I

remember you laughed because you thought I was joking."

Valerie coughed again but this time blood leaked from her mouth. "Valerie please...hang in there...we are almost home."

Ray sat on the couch drinking a bottle of beer thinking about how losing her scared him. It was the first time he was afraid. He only ever said those words once before in his life thinking he would never say them again.

"Why do you look like that?" Valerie asked while touching his back as they sat on the beach at night looking at the moon's reflection on the water. "Talk to me..."

Ray got up and paced back and forth nervous. Valerie was concerned she had never seen him nervous before. "Ray? You are scaring me..."

"No, I'm not going to say it." Ray said to himself, "No…"
Valerie looked at him pacing, "Say what?"
"I'm just going to do it." Ray stopped pacing and stood in front of her. "Stand up."
Valerie stood up facing him, "Okay" she laughed.
"I have something to say to you."
"You are scaring me mister."
"I am falling in love with you Valerie," Ray said while looking at her.
Valerie froze…

Liam walked into the kitchen to get some water. Ray pointed his gun but stopped when he saw Liam. "Whoa!?" Liam said while throwing up his hands, "It's just me."

"My bad" Ray said while lowering his weapon.

"You good? You look like you were deep in thought."

"I do love your sister. I have for years," Ray confessed, "When she was shot I thought I had lost her for good."

Liam walked over to the living room, "So what happened?"

"She uh, she didn't remember much of anything when she woke up from coma. So I just kept an eye on her from a far."

"You wanted to keep her safe."

Ray nodded, "Yea. What people don't understand was things with Val was draining at times. No matter how much you love someone if the situation isn't right, it won't work."

Liam nodded and began to exit the room but before he did, "She still loves you ya know. I saw it in her eyes when you kissed her. Every emotion she has is seen in her eyes that's why she doesn't make eye contact that often."

Ray laughed at that fact because he knew that about Val. She struggled with eye contact because it always showed how she felt about him. Valerie wasn't afraid to show pain, anger, or frustration…just love. "Thanks."

"Good night."

Valerie laid in bed tossing and turning as sweat rolled down her face from her mind working in over time.

"This is the lay out of the house…" Valerie said while expanding the schematics on the screen, "We have to land at least a couple miles back." Ray leaned over her lightly brushing against her as he touched the screen,

"Exactly. You're right. So three men can take the right and you and the other members can take the left."

"Sounds like a plan." Valerie smiled. Ray looked at her and whispered, "They can see you smiling at me." Valerie got close to his face, "I know." She walked away and looked at Jason, another teammate texting on his phone. Lucas jumped out in front of her, "So can we count on you to join the mission."

"Yea, I just told Ray I would go."

"Good, I was beginning to worry that you would sit this one out. I need my best on this mission." Lucas explained.

"No worries." As Valerie walked away she heard Lucas's voice talking to someone, "It's a go."

"Yes sir" the person answered. Valerie turned around and saw Jason nodding and walking away from Lucas. She scrunched her face but blew off the words.

COLUMBIA

"Okay lets knock this one out. Jason you take overwatch and the six of us will handle down low." Ray yelled over the sound of the truck coming to a stop to let them off. "We got one shot to get this guy!"

"I am going after the target!" Valerie yelled and took off running.

"Valerie! Valerie!" Ray yelled back. He turned to Jason, "Keep watch. Take point up there on those hills."

"Yes sir" Jason smiled. Jason ran to the top of the nearby hill and loaded up his sniper rifle. He pressed the button on his bluetooth, "I am in position sir." Back at the agency Lucas nodded, "Good. Remember take Valerie out."

"I understand sir."

"Are you sure you can make the shot."

"Do you doubt me sir?" Jason asked. Lucas leaned back in his leather office chair, "Do I doubt your abilities? No, *but the one person who I am confident can make the shot is the person we are going to kill."*

"Just consider it done."

"Then the money will be waiting for you when you land back in the states." *Valerie climbed the wall to the balcony as the rain pour down wetting her clothes and hair. She paused when she saw Santos through the glass doors staring back at her.*

"Target in sight..." Jason said into the bluetooth. He fired two shots and watched her drop. "It's done sir."

"Good. Now clear out and tell Ray you didn't make it to the hill because you were nearly ambushed. Understand?"

"Yes sir."

Valerie jumped up her eyes wide from shock. Her hair was drenched from sweat as she pushed a few strains away from her face. Casper lightly knocked on the door, "You okay?"

"What gave you the idea I wasn't?"

"You were talking in your sleep."

Valerie climbed out of bed and walked past her to the bathroom to rinse off her face, "I am fine."

"So I am guessing that you dreamt something."

Valerie looked at Casper in the mirror, "Jason was the shooter, and Lucas set this whole thing up. Ray told Jason to take overwatch."

"Jason…" Casper thought, "How in the hell did he make that shot?"

"I don't know, but I am going to find out." Valerie said while going back to the bedroom to get dressed.

"Wait, you are going to find him tonight!? Whoa slow yourself girl, you were already nearly killed once today."

"I don't care, that bastard shot me in the back twice. I want answers as to why." Valerie grabbed her gun and jacket, "Find him."

"Alright, I will get his last known address." Casper went to her computer and started typing, "Are you going to kill him?"

Valerie cut her eyes at Casper's stupid question that had an obvious answer. "Okay, so how about we try to get information first before spooking him." Casper suggested.

"Casper…"

"Valerie!" Casper yelled, "I um don't yell but I am yelling. I am not a field operative, but I do know that if you don't get as much as you can…he could go back to Lucas before we even finish saving the city."

Valerie smiled, "I am just going to get some answers. Don't worry when I'm done he won't be doing anymore talking." She looked at the computer and grabbed her keys.

"I am sure of it." Casper whispered under her breath as Valerie shut the door to head towards the elevator.

Jason lived closer to the woods and lake area part of California. He originally built a cabin out there away from things. Right as Jason opened the cabinet to grab a plate for his food the power went out. The cabin went black. Immediately he knew it was Valerie, because it was only a matter of time before her memory pieced things together. Lucas covered the paper trail but her suspicion was enough to believe Jason was the shooter.

Jason pulled a pistol out of his kitchen drawer, "I know that's you Val...!"

He slowly crept down the hallway towards the back living room. The second he turned the corner Valerie punched him in the face. "I see your memory has come back!" Jason said while grabbing his nose that was now dripping blood.

"Just enough to know it was you who shot me." Valerie swung and he blocked her punch and wrapped his arm around her neck trying to choke her.

"I carried out an order! Did you forget what that was like?" Jason said while tightening his arm around her neck. Valerie broke one arm free and elbow punched him in the abdomen repeatedly before breaking free. "I don't take orders that means blindly killing my teammates."

"That's not true!" Jason tackled her and the two crashed into the coffee table. Valerie flipped over and kicked him in the face while bending his arm back. Snap! She broke his arm. "Ahhhh!!!" Jason yelled while climbing up the couch to regain strength. Valerie jumped and punch him in the face knocking him out. He fell back and she stood over him.

10 minutes later Jason woke up while being tied to a chair. "Hello," Valerie said in a smart tone while holding her gun.

"I won't talk Val, you should know you won't get anything out of me." Jason was confident he could withstand any torturing she would try. Valerie shot him in the knee and he screamed out in pain.

"It was a bad choice to live in such a remote area. No one can hear you scream." Valerie said, "You and I need talk."

"Too late?" Jason looked around and sniffed the air, "What is that smell?"

"Gasoline."

"Valerie...Val..."

"Did Lucas set me up?" Valerie asked.

"Valerie..." Jason pleaded. In response she pressed the gun against his other knee, "Tell me!!" she yelled.

"Yes! Okay, yes Lucas gave me $200,000 extra to take you out on the Columbia mission."

"Why?"

"I don't know!" Jason yelled with panic.

Valerie shot his other knee, "I am running out of patience...why Jason!?" "Something about covering up another mission from two years prior. But that is all I know!!" Jason answered as spit dripped from his mouth.

"What mission!! You're lying and I am sick and tired of people lying to me!!" Valerie yelled in his face. She walked over to the wall and lit a match, "I drop this and you plus your little cabin will go up in flames."

"Prague! But I swear Valerie I don't know anything else!" Jason yelled.

Valerie smirked, "I believe you." She tossed the match on him and his body caught fire. She walked out of the cabin and through the woods to her vehicle parked miles away. Slowly the cabin caught fire and Valerie stop to take one look back. The cabin burned down.

*"Bravo 1 take the shot if you have it,"
Lucas commanded over the radio. Ray
covered the radio and grabbed Lucas,
"I don't think she can make a long
range sniper shot like that!"
Lucas shook his head, "I believe she
can."
"What is it with you and her? It is like
you want her to become this dangerous
person."
Lucas sat down the radio, "Not a
dangerous person Ray. I want her to
become a dangerous weapon. One that
the enemy will regret meeting."
Ray squinted his eyes and stepped back,
"I wonder what your goals are
sometimes Lucas."
"My goals are to protect this country
and its agenda. What is yours?" Lucas*

said while picking back up the radio.
"Bravo 1?"
Valerie who was nearly 1000 meters
away on a hill looking through the
scope on the sniper rifle. She was
breathing slowly, and pulled the trigger.
"Target neutralized," she responded.
Lucas looked at Ray, "and you did a
damn good job training her."
Ray took a deep breath. He was in love
with someone who struggled with her
own skills. Valerie was and will be one
of the best they have ever taught.

Ray slowly opened his eyes to see
Valerie sitting in front of him with blood
stains on her torn clothes. "Valerie!?"
Ray said while touching her face, "You
found…"

"Jason" she finished. For a moment she
was in a daze. Was she becoming the
person she always was or someone

different. "I can't remember the last time I wasn't afraid to kill someone."

Ray took a deep breath, "Jason is dead."

Valerie nodded, "I wasn't afraid."

"You never were Valerie. I trained you not to be." Ray said while handing her his bottle of water. He took her into his arms and held her while kissing her forehead. "You are beginning to become the person you once were."

"I am a killer," Valerie whispered.

"Yes, one the government used on countless missions."

Valerie looked into his eyes, "what do you see me as? Who am I to you?"

"You are the woman I fell in love with. Despite the training and skills there is a side of you that no one else sees but me."

Valerie nodded as she laid back down into his arms, "Lucas is behind all of this Ray. He is the last name on my list."

"Was I ever on your list?" Ray asked scared she was concentrating on the fact that he could have been involved in her set up.

"You were." Valerie said while closing her eyes.

Ray walked in on Valerie training. She was one of the few operatives always training, preparing, and learning. It was her goal to be the best at the job. Valerie lowered the knife and looked at Ray who was leaning against the door entrance smiling at her. "You are always the first one here and the last one to leave."

Valerie nodded, "and you are the only one who works as hard as I do."

"Of course, I trained you."

Valerie flipped the knife and pointed the handle towards Ray, "Care to join me?"

Ray walked over and grabbed the knife as the two squared off. He swung the knife at her and she dodged the swing, "you missed!"

Ray swept her leg, caught her, and held the knife to her neck, "I don't miss Val."

Valerie took a deep breath and looked down at his side. He followed her eye line and saw she had a smaller hand knife pointed at his stomach, "Neither do I," she responded.

Ray helped her stand up straight and nodded, "I see you have surpassed me."

"I couldn't do that."

"Valerie you are great at being in the field. Directly involved in the action. I am good at training and teaching. We

both have our strengths," Ray said while flipping the knife and handing it back to her.

Valerie took the knife threw it directly into the wall, "I guess you're right."
She walked over to gather her things and zip up her bag. "Don't let this job get to you," Ray said.
Valerie looked at him, "Get to me?"
"You risk breaking faster than you think if you do. Keep some of your humanity, one mission at a time."

"Good morning, I had no idea you were here," Liam said while walking into the kitchen to see his sister sitting at the table.

"Morning, I came late last night."

Liam looked at his sister stare outside with a blank look. He tried to assess her emotions in the silence between them, "You okay?"

Valerie nodded, "I am."

"Val…"

"Liam…I am fine," she said while getting up, "You should get ready. The office is expecting us."

"Right, I forgot that after nearly getting killed I still have to go to work."

"Ironic isn't it." Valerie patted him on the back, "I am going to go change, can I ride with you?"

"Sure."

Casper who had just walked in followed Valerie to the guest room, "Does your brother know you killed someone last night?"

"Nope, and I would like to keep it that way."

Casper shrugged, "Okay, but I am sure he will figure out how crazy you really are in due time." Valerie looked at her for a second before going back to sifting through dresses to wear. Casper reached out and grabbed her wrist, and within a millisecond Valerie had a knife to her neck.

"Whoa!!!!" Casper yelled while releasing her and lifting her hands, "I was just going to ask if you were mentally okay…"

Valerie lowered the knife, "I am sorry. I am on edge."

"I can see. Damn you nearly cut my throat!"

"Casper," Valerie whispered fighting back tears, "My mind is chaotic. It is mixed with violence, anger, revenge, pain, hurt, and love."

"You have to take this one day at a time. To be honest I knew you returning was a bad idea."

Valerie nodded, "But once I started figuring things out I couldn't ignore the facts."

"and is Ray involved in this? Did you figure that out?"

"I did," Valerie answered, "I think I still love him."

"I figured that too," Casper said while sitting on the bed, "But you can't." Valerie nodded, "I can't."

"Look, your brother needs you. The city needs you, focus your efforts on that right now and finish this." Casper suggested.

"Thank you, I don't know what I would do without your help."

Casper stood up ready to hug her but stopped in her tracks, "I am about to hug you. You don't have any secret tools, knives, guns or anything?"

Valerie laughed and hugged her, "I wouldn't hurt you Casper, you're my friend."

"Good."

Ray knocked on the door, "Morning. Um, Valerie are you ready to move?"

"Let me slip into my dress." Valerie said while walking to the bathroom and shutting the door. Casper looked at Ray and squinted her eyes.

"What's that look for?"

Casper walked over to him, "You still love her."

Ray was about to talk but Casper cut him off, "No need to answer. Just know that it can't happen this time. You two are in a worldwide situation that requires her to focus. She is fragile and you poking that part of her brain doesn't help."

Ray took a deep breath, "Is this you acting on behalf of her as her friend?"

"This is me acting as her friend, and her analyst that doesn't want her killed in the field."

"Fair enough."

Valerie walked out in another tight forrest green knee length dress and black pumps, "I am ready." Ray stopped mid-thought when he saw her. Valerie laughed, "Don't look at me like that."

"My fault, um Liam and I will be downstairs."

Casper shook her head, "You two are the weirdest people I know."

"That is very true."

Liam and Valerie shared the car ride while Casper and Ray found a local spot to park nearby. This was the day that Santos and his crew planned on making their move on the treasury and the city. In the car Valerie was looking at the map of the corner block with the new development and treasury. "Liam, what is this passage here?"

"That is a tunnel that the city sealed off five years ago to keep the water ways from flooding the block. Why?" Liam asked while driving.

"I think he is using this as his entrance. He knows we are coming, so he will probably plant the explosives there. Ray!"

"Go" Ray answered while glancing at Casper.

"We need back up down here now." Valerie demanded.

"I will get on it."

Liam parked the car and looked at his sister, "What do you need me to do?"

"I need you to evacuate the city block. Get the police to remove these people reporting the bomb threat." Valerie explained while grabbing her bag and pulling out a gun.

"Valerie that will cause an uproar."

"I know, but Santos doesn't care."

Liam nodded and got out of the car, as soon as the door shut Valerie changed clothes and got out the car, "talk to me Casper."

"Six men were spotted three blocks away, and shots have been fired." Casper said while typing. She looked at Ray who was loading his gun, "Let her know I am headed down there now."

"Ray is on his way" Casper complied.

"Good, because I am going into the thick of it." Valerie said while taking off running as people were screaming in fear and running helplessly. Santos and his crew entered the tunnels as a second group broke off to cause havoc and distractions in the streets.

Ray was speeding through traffic to get downtown as fast as he could. "Ray I need you to get to Liam and help him get as many people out of the city block." Valerie said over the comms.

"You love giving directions, I thought that was my job," Ray answered.

Valerie stopped before looking at a secondary tunnel entrance, "It is but for now…"

"I got him, just be careful."

Casper went into the agency and sat down at the analyst desk to begin typing. The entire analyst team was on alert and working helplessly to prevent the attack.

Lucas walked into the room and stood behind Casper, "I am guessing my two best agents are downtown right now."

"You guess right."

"How did things get this far without me being filled in?"

Casper spun her chair around to look at him, "Do you want the answer to that or do you want me to help them prevent thousands of people from dying?"

Lucas stared back at her as she squinted her eyes at him, "Help them, but this conversation isn't over. I want 15 minute updates, understand?"

"Got it boss." Casper said while typing, "Alright Valerie I am getting schematics of the tunnel. Looks like city block cameras have Santos right hand and a few men entering the west side of the tunnel."

"Casper, city police are on site" another analyst yelled.

"Ray do you copy?"

Ray was on the sidewalk evacuating people with Liam, "I got it, but I can't find the men who were shooting!"

Casper was typing accessing more city cameras and saw four men entering the treasury building, "The treasury building Ray."

"Got it." Ray rushed over to Liam, "Take this…" he said while handing him a gun.

"What?! I don't know how to use…"

Ray cut him off, "Learn." He left Liam standing with a few people as he ran towards the treasury building.

Valerie was slowly moving through lagging tunnel water as she held her gun in her hands. Part of her felt like her old self, but another piece was afraid. As she turned the corner she saw the cement blocker in the tunnel covered with C4 explosives. "Damn…" she whispered, "Casper…"

"Yea Val?"

"There is enough C4 down here to take out the city block," Valerie responded. Ray stopped by the side door after hearing about the bomb, "Valerie you can't stay down there. We don't know who has the trigger."

"My guess is Santos." Valerie commented, "I can take pictures and you can help me try to disarm it."

"Okay, I am waiting for uploads." Casper said.

Ray shook his head, "Valerie, let me disarm the bomb and you come to the treasury."

"Ray…I will handle this. Stay where you are." Valerie said in a trembling voice as she took pictures of the bomb to upload to Casper. Valerie slowly lowered the phone as she felt the end of gun press against her head.

"Put the phone down, and take out your weapon," Marquez said in a low voice.

Valerie did as he asked and slowly lifted her hands while turning around. "I should have been the one to kill you in

Columbia." Marquez commented. As Valerie turned around she moved her arm knocking the gun out of his hand and punching him with the other, "You're right, you should've killed me."

Marquez wiped his lip with his hand, "Nice punch, but you will have to do better than that princess," he swung back punching her. He picked her up and slammed her against the brick wall. "Ahhhh!!!" Valerie screamed while elbowing him in the shoulders trying to break free. Marquez threw her against the other side of the tunnel, "Get up!!!" He yelled.

Valerie slowly got up. Marquez pulled out a knife and the two continued fighting each other. Valerie flipped over him, kicked his knee and put him in a choke hold. She pulled her arms as tight as she could as Marquez was 6 foot and muscular.

Meanwhile, Ray took out the men in the treasury working with local authorities before noticing he hadn't heard anything from Valerie. "Casper, any word on Val?" He asked.

"No, but Ray I am hearing fighting and screaming. She isn't alone in the tunnel."

Ray took off running, "Direct me to the nearest entrance." Without noticing him, Liam followed behind Ray hoping to find his little sister.

"Take the west entrance of the tunnel," Casper directed.

Marquez broke the choke hold and cut Valerie on her side. She backed up while touching the wound. Marquez flipped the knife pointing it back at her, "You are mixed up in something you have no idea how deep it goes."

"Why don't you enlighten me."

"You think we just magically gained access to everything and knew where to break in and plant bombs? It is your agency!" Marquez shouted.

Valerie squinted her eyes wondering why he was sharing this information, "You're lying," she double punched him and kicked him in the face. He fell back.

Marquez spit out some blood and shook his head, "You Americans are so stupid. You blindly trust the same people who are quietly betraying you." He slid his hand over to grab his gun and pointed it at her. Valerie backed up and Marquez shot her in the upper thigh. "Ah!" Valerie cried out in pain from the wound. The bullet went straight through.

"Like I said," Marquez continued, "You people are stupid." He pulled out the black trigger and started the timer counting down from 3 minutes. Marquez pressed the gun against the center of Valerie's forehead, "You were the one person we needed to take out."

"Why?"

"Because it was your mission that brought you guys to Columbia." Marquez noted, "Oh that's right, you have memory issues."

Within seconds a bullet went through Marquez's head and he fell to the ground. Valerie sighed with relief to look over and see Ray holding the gun. He ran over to her, "Are you okay?"

"Oh it's just a stab wound and gun shot wound. I am good babe." Valerie joked.

Ray shook his head, "you always make a joke when you're uncomfortable."

Liam interrupted the moment and ran over, "Valerie!"

"Liam, what are you doing down here?" Valerie said while looking at him then at Ray.

"I followed him."

Valerie looked over at the bomb, "We can't stay down here, this bomb is going to go off."

"Good idea, lets get you out of here" Ray went to pick her up and Valerie backed up.

"No…" Valerie started, "Casper will walk me through disarming this. Take my brother an get out of here now!"

"Valerie don't be stupid!" Liam shouted. Valerie walked over to her brother, "I love you brother, you need to go."

"Valerie," Ray started, "I am not leaving you."

Valerie picked up the knife, "Casper we have seconds left I need to know how to disarm this."

"Valerie!!!" Ray shouted, "Look at me, we all need to leave!"

"Ray," Valerie turned around, "I love you. I never stopped. I know you love me too. So get my brother out of here, now!!!!"

Liam slowly started backing up and Ray stared at Valerie. Holding the eye contact as she saw sadness in his eyes of possibly losing her. "I am right behind you guys." She whispered.

Ray took off running with Liam as she turned her attention back to the bomb. "Alright Casper."

"Valerie you have 7 seconds left." Casper said, "We don't have enough time."

Valerie sighed, "I know."

Ray and Liam made it out of the tunnel sprinting and making sure the block was evacuated within seconds the bomb exploded and the development crumbled. Ray and Liam fell back as they saw the explosion and dust fill the air. "NO!!!" Liam yelled. Ray sat up as his eyes widen from realizing that Valerie was gone.

Back at the agency Casper took off her head set and threw it across the desk in anger. Lucas walked in, "Update?"

"People are safe. One agent cleared, the other possibly dead."

"Valerie?" Lucas asked.

Casper stood up, "Wouldn't you like that."

"Excuse me?"

"She knows! Whatever that means to you, know that Valerie knew you were the one behind the shooting." Casper said while walking off.

Lucas stood in the room and relief fell on him as he exhaled believing he got away with it all. He walked out of the analyst room and dialed a number on his phone. A male voice answered on the other end. "I thought I told you not to call me again until you have resolved the matter."

"I did sir. She is terminated." Lucas confirmed.

"Good."

"Chief!?" Lucas said before the male could hang up, "What about Santos?"

"I took care of him. He is headed back to Columbia now. There are bigger matters on our hands. If anyone finds out about what happened in Prague…"

"They won't sir."

"Keep it that way." The male said before hanging up.

Liam sat in the back of an ambulance as he watched first responders make their way into the rubble. Ray walked over to him, "She isn't coming back Liam."

"I know." Liam said in a monotone voice. Distraught from the fact of losing his sister. "She said she loved you."

Ray nodded, "Your sister and I were lovers. For years we kept what we had a secret."

"Are…" Liam corrected, "Are lovers, I saw the way you looked at her down there."

Ray took a deep breath, "I never thought I would love anyone else, but then I met her. If you ever need anything…let me know. I promised her I would be here to help you."

"What do I tell my parents!?" Liam asked.

"This is where the lying starts Liam. You tell them she went back into the military and died on a mission over seas." Ray answered.

Lucas was in a warehouse securing the $3 million dollars he stole during the Columbia mission. Eric walked in, "Brother!"

"I thought I told you to get out of town!?" Lucas shouted, "I help fake your death so no one would look for you and connect this whole thing."

"I want the money you promised me."

"I will wire you some money, but do us a both a favor and get on the next plane to a country with no extradition treaty." Lucas pleaded. His phone buzzed showing a message: **#iRemember - Valerie**

Lucas was confused while staring at the message that arrived from an unknown number. "She is supposed to be dead…" he whispered to himself.

"Who is?" Eric asked.

"Eric leave now!!!" Lucas shouted.

Eric nodded at his brother as he made his way to his car to leave the warehouse. Lucas's phone lit up showing 'unknown'. "Hello?" Lucas answered.

"You thought I was dead?" Valerie's voice chimed in.

"I was hoping."

"Wrong." Valerie said while looking through the sniper rifle scope and shot Lucas in the back through the ware house window. She hung up the phone and made her way down to the entrance.

Lucas fell to the ground as he felt the sharp pain in his back.

Valerie walked in to see him on his knees. Her thigh bandaged up and a pistol in her hand, "Eric is your brother…"

Lucas nodded, "Yes…why didn't you do a kill shot."

"I wanted to show you I am still good. Plus we still need to talk." Valerie said while punching him in the face. "What did Marquez mean by the mission in Prague?"

Lucas was coughing with his face in the dirt, "I see when we shot you that head injury did more damage than expected."

Valerie kicked him and shot him in the leg, "Do not patronize me!"

"How can you not remember Prague!! You killed over 15 people there!" Lucas shouted.

"For what?"

"Ray! You went on a rescue mission for Ray!" Lucas explained. "Stupid relationship."

Valerie shook her head, "I killed 15 people for Ray."

"What? You find it hard to believe that you would do anything for the man you are in love with? Please!" Lucas fussed while lying in the dirt, "I figured you two out with no problem. All your arguing and swooning."

Valerie kneeled down and grabbed his neck. Lucas looked into her eyes, "I am glad you got the head injury because the one person you didn't remember was him. Maybe that is why it was so easy for Eric to get into your pants." Lucas added.

Valerie started punching him repeatedly. Her anger was making her lose control, but she knew she needed answers and killing Lucas right away wouldn't help. She backed up and pointed the gun at him. "Do it Valerie! Be the killer I always knew you were!"

"There is more to Prague than just a rescue mission," Valerie commented.

"You're right. There is much more to all of this than you will ever know!"

Valerie lowered the gun and walked over to Lucas, "I won't kill you. The agency is aware of what you've done and they are on the way to arrest you."

Lucas's eyes widen in fear. Valerie smiled, "Now that is the look I was hoping for. I don't know who you are answering to but my guess is they won't like that you were shot and beat up by the person you were hoping was dead."

"You bi…"

Valerie shot him in the arm, "Shut your mouth!! I will figure all of this out and take down anyone involved in trying to kill me. Jason is dead, you're going to prison or wherever they want to stick you, and whomever is next!"

"Valerie!!!! Valerie!!!!" Lucas shouted as she walked away.

Valerie got in the car and drove away. "A team is on their way." Casper chimed in on the communications, "Glad you're not dead."

"I may not be dead but I am in pain."
Valerie said while fighting her wounds.

"Valerie, I found something else you
should know…" Casper added.

"What?"

"Ray, what he was writing in his reports
about you. It isn't good." Casper shared
worried how she would react to the
information, "I know you two…"

Valerie pursed her lips, "What does it
say?"

"What they say, he has stuff written
about you in more than one. He called
you intolerable, he doesn't like working
with you, he can't be on a team with
you. He also told other team members to
watch their backs with you." Casper was
reading, as she had hacked the file
system to pull up more information.

Valerie slammed on breaks in shock. The sound of Casper talking drowned out as Valerie questioned everything about Ray. How could he be with her in secret and say those things about her. "Valerie…Valerie!!" Casper shouted, "I know what you're thinking…"

"I want to see the reports."

"Okay, are you sure?"

"Yes. I also need tickets to Prague so I can finish finding out who set me up. This is much deeper than Lucas and Eric."

"I will work on it." Casper responded.

Ray was in his home drinking hard liquor on the rocks at the kitchen table. He was thinking heavily about Valerie.

The memory of the two of them popped in his mind.

"You were there during my darkest hour," Ray said while lying his head on Valerie's chest. Valerie caressed his head, "I am always here for you."
"I know and I am appreciative of you. No one knows what I've been through."
"Why tell me?" Valerie asked.
Ray lifted his head, "you were there when no one else was…"

"Do you mind patching me up…" Valerie interrupted while leaning against the wall bleeding. She nearly fainted before Ray caught her in his arms. "Valerie!"

"Oh my gosh Ray…" Valerie said while untying him and helping him down from hanging from the ceiling. He was heavy and she struggled to hold him up, "Can you walk?"

Ray nodded, "I can…"

Valerie froze when she heard men speaking German coming from the hallway. She looked at Ray, "I am going to get you out of here."

"Valerie wait! I need to get the black box." Ray fussed while regaining his strength.

"Ray what box!? We need to go now." Valerie pulled out her gun to reload the magazine. "I am here to save you and I have transport waiting for us."

"That black box is critical to this mission."

Valerie touched his face, "Then you should have thought about that before you got caught! We are leaving now!!"

Valerie woke up gasping for air as her body ached in pain from the wounds. She groaned as she rolled on her side to see Ray was sitting on the coffee table to hand her some hot tea, "Drink this…"

"Thank you," she said while sipping from the mug, "Were you watching me sleep?"

Ray nodded, "I wasn't sure if you were going to wake up."

"You weren't sure I was even alive."

"I had a small feeling but I didn't want to get my hopes up."

"Good because I wasn't sure if I was coming here."

"Valerie, you mumbled something," Ray started, "While you were sleeping you mentioned a black box."

Valerie's eyes sharpened her look at him as she sat upright on the couch. She waited to see if his statement would follow with something else. "What do you know about a black box?" He continued.

"I don't know anything. I barely remembered anything from Columbia Ray."

Ray nodded, she could see he didn't completely accept her answer. "What do you know about a black box?" She asked in return.

Ray looked at her, "There is no black box Valerie." He got up and walked to grab a hand towel for her to wipe her face.

"…and Prague?" Valerie wasn't giving up that he knew more than he was saying.

"Small mission, nothing serious." Ray finished. He touched her face and lightly kissed her, "Can we just stop and focus on the fact that I almost lost you."

Valerie nodded, "I know."

"Don't ever scare me like that again."

She kissed him again and smiled, "I won't."

"Come on, lets go upstairs and get some rest. It has been a long night." Ray said while standing up and holding out his hand to receive hers.

Valerie placed her hand in his and followed him upstairs to the bedroom. The two slept peacefully for a few hours before Valerie opened her eyes. She knew he was lying to her but now the question is why. Light fog filled the night air and Valerie snuck out of bed to gather her things. She took one last look at him sleeping before she walked down the stairs and out the door to meet a car that was waiting.

She got in the passenger side and looked at Casper, "Thank you for coming to get me."

"A call from my friend in the wee hours of the night...no problem." Casper said as they drove off. "Mind telling me what's going on?"

"Did you find any information on our mission in Prague?" Valerie asked.

Casper handed her an envelop, "This was all I could dig up."

"Ray lied to me," Valerie started, "I don't know why except that he is hiding something."

Casper handed Valerie a second envelop, "These are his reports Val..."

Valerie pulled out the papers and skim through the paragraphs to see key words, "It sounds like he hates me."

"Yea, which confuses me because you two were just lying in bed together. He was persistent in being there for you, so how can he hate you this much to say all these things behind your back?" Casper asked.

Valerie sighed, "I don't know Casper. When you are trying to protect yourself you will do whatever is necessary." She ripped the papers into smaller pieces and stuffed them back in the envelope before tossing it in the back seat.

"Do you think he is part of something bigger?"

Valerie looked at her, "I hope not."

"I think as much as you are mad and hurt, you still love him. So you killing him doesn't sound like an option."

Valerie shook her head, "I wouldn't. He is the one person I try not to hurt, and there are a few times I failed at that."

"Valerie," Casper said with dismay, "Maybe you should talk to him."

Valerie stuff the other envelops in her bag, "Talking got me no where, just shot in the back leaving me with no one to trust. A husband who lied to me, an agency director who was part of the plan, and a lover who lied to me. They shouldn't have missed their shot. Now, they won't see me coming."

Casper got onto the interstate leading to the airport, "Are you sure you want to go to Prague?"

"I need answers Casper. This is deeper than Columbia and I am at the center of it all."

"Valerie, you go up against Ray things could get real between you two. Are you sure you can do what is necessary when the time calls for it because I am thinking he has the same dilemma."

Valerie couldn't answer. She knew that if it came down to her and Ray pointing a gun at one another she wouldn't know what to feel or do. Part of her feels he would pull the trigger first, but deep down they would just stand off daring the other to make a move.

"I will cross that bridge when I come to it."

Casper nodded in agreement, "Okay."

"Ray and I didn't anticipate getting to this place. The backstabbing, and lies between the two of us. This isn't an easy fix anymore." Valerie looked out the window, "everyone doesn't know that everyone knows."

Casper pulled up to the terminal and handed Val one last envelop, "Passport, cash, and burner phone. This is everything you need to get there. Valerie, your family thinks you're dead…"

"I need it to stay that way. If this is as big as I think, I don't need them in danger. Just keep an eye on my brother for me, please."

Casper agreed, "I have a bad feeling about this."

Valerie got out of the car, "You always do."

As Valerie walked through the entrance of the airport to get tickets she glanced back at Casper who had fear in her eyes. Valerie knew that Casper was concerned about the outcome, two strong agents with a past love battling each other. But, in order to find the truth it meant retracing the past.

Meanwhile, Ray was sitting up in his bed shirtless while holding his phone to his ear. "Sir…we have a problem."

"What now?" A male voice said on the other end.

"Valerie, her memory is coming back."

"Are you sure of this?"

Ray sighed, "I am sir. She may not tell me but I know her very well."

"Then you know what you must do."

"Sir, she mentioned the black box. I believe she is going after it."

"Then you go after her. I need this shut down now Ray! No mistakes!"

Ray's voice trembled as he answered, "Yes sir."

"Ray…" the male voice said, "Lucas failed. You better not do the same."

Ray sighed while looking at the chain Valerie gave him and a gun lying next to it, "I won't sir." He ended the call and laid his phone back on the night stand. His brain rattling through memories.

Valerie caressed his face and kissed him, "I won't hurt you."
"You sure of that?"

"I promise" Valerie said while looking deep into his eyes, "I don't make promises I won't keep."
"Good, because I wouldn't hurt you either."

Ray got up and grabbed a travel bag from his closet and started grabbing clothes. He pulled out a lower compartment in his closet to reveal passports, money, and maps.

Valerie waited as the clerk printed her ticket, "Where are you headed?" She asked.

"Prague." Valerie said with a small smile, "I have history there."

The clerk handed her the ticket and smiled, "Well safe travels and enjoy your flight."

"Thank you." Valerie said while walking through the terminal.

2 Weeks Later

Valerie slowly opened her eyes to see herself in a dark cold room. She went to move her body and cringed from a healing wound. She lightly ran her fingers across the fresh stitches. An old man walked in and held up both hands for her not to move. He spoke German to her and Valerie squinted her eyes. Her eyes scattered as she without thought responded…

"Please be careful you are still healing," the man said while giving her some water.

Valerie responded, "Where am I?"

"Amsterdam…my ugh my wife found you in the ally way. You were stabbed.

We thought someone robbed you or something." He explained.

Valerie dug into her pockets and found a key with a flip phone. "I need to go…" she said while getting up and grabbing her clothes.

"Wait!" The man said while slowly holding up a nine millimeter gun, "We found this on you too."

Valerie put on her jacket and took the gun, "Thank you."

She walked out the home and onto the street. She dug into her jacket pocket and found a hotel room key. She decided to head back there hoping to retrace her steps. Things started in Prague and now she is Amsterdam, but what happened?

The flip phone buzzed and she answered, "Casper?"

"Valerie! Thank God I have been calling and when I got no answer I thought you were dead."

"Not yet" Valerie said.

"I told you to be careful digging into this issue alone. The agency is looking for you, and I think they sent Ray."

"Well I lost the last two weeks and I have a stab wound so I must be headed down the right path." Valerie responded sarcastically. She kept looking over her shoulder because she felt she was being followed.

"Valerie…" Casper said into the phone. Valerie stopped walking when she heard a noise behind her. Looking to her left and right she turned down a side road and stood against the wall.

"Casper I gotta go," immediately Val ended the call.

Casper stared at her phone watching the words 'call ended' on the screen, "Valerie," she said under her breath. She tossed the phone and got up from her desk to walk down the main hallway. She stopped when she saw a man in a navy blue suit, clean shaved, 6'1 greet other administrators.

Valerie took two deep breaths, "I knew you would find me!"

Ray's voice broke through the shadows, "We have unfinished business."

Valerie slowly pulled out her gun and was trigger ready, "You're right."

"Valerie let me take you in!" Ray shouted.

Valerie stepped out the shadows and pointed her gun straight at Ray who had his gun pointed back at her. "No," she said sternly while staring at him.

"When will you trust me?" Ray asked while lightly touching his finger to the trigger.

"I don't trust someone who has done as much as you have behind my back." Valerie said while gripping the trigger.

Flash backs flew threw their minds as they were reminded of their intense connection. It was either they honestly hated one another, hated that they had feelings for one another, or struggled with their feelings that constantly pulled them off a certain path.

"Obviously, I am nothing to you! Just some teammate you have slept with!" Valerie shouted at him.

Ray turned around and walked across the room to her, "Don't say that! You know the power you have over me, how you make me feel. You're more than a damn quickie."

Valerie stood in his face deeply taking in each breath as he moved in to kiss her but pulled back. He repeated himself, "Don't ever say that again."

"Then what am I to you Ray?" Valerie asked. She felt herself giving up trying to understand what the two of them shared.

"Don't make me do this Val...please," Ray pleaded while closing the gap between them, "You're already injured."

"Injured Ray. Not dead." Valerie said while tightening her grip on her weapon, "I'm not going back until I have answers."

"Valerie!"

"Ray!!"

Two shots…."Pop, Pop."